The Cottage

The Cottage

Donna Vamplew

iUniverse LLC
Bloomington

THE COTTAGE

iUniverse books may be ordered through booksellers or by contacting:

iUniverse LLC
1663 Liberty Drive
Bloomington, IN 47403
www.iuniverse.com
1-800-Authors (1-800-288-4677)

ISBN: 978-1-4917-0719-7 (sc)
ISBN: 978-1-4917-0720-3 (e)

Library of Congress Control Number: 2013916944

Printed in the United States of America.

iUniverse rev. date: 10/02/2013

When Michael Ryan
came to the cottage,
it changed
Elizabeth's world.

Two different worlds.
Two different people.

What do you trust?
Your instincts
or
your brain?

To my mother, Alfreda Marchand,
who taught me how to write and how to dream!

Acknowledgments

My mother did not follow her dreams.
She made the best with what she had!

But she never denied my right to dream.

This book is the attainment of one of my dreams.

I acknowledge my husband's faith in me
and his never-ending ability to dream.
He is forever following his dreams.
I am now following one of mine.

This is a story about a man and a woman.

**A good man and a good woman
can make dreams come true.**

Chapter 1

May 3, 2004

Elizabeth knew her understudy could take her place and perform beautifully.

There is no need to feel guilty; no one is indispensable. That's what she had to keep telling herself as she drove toward the old cottage. No phones, no TV, no computers— silence! That's what she needed. Silence. Her mind needed it, and her body needed it.

When she was almost at the turnoff to the cottage, she saw a lot of motorcycles on the shoulder. She thought she had come upon an accident. She soon saw that, instead, it looked like some kind of confrontation. The idea of a group of motorcycle gang members realizing that she had come upon their "business" petrified her, especially with all the blood she saw on the side of the road. As she hurried by, she noticed that one man was getting beat up. A few men were holding him, and a few men were hitting him.

None of your business. Keep going! Go to the cottage.

It had been a long time since she'd experienced the serenity and security of the old cottage. She desperately needed her grandmother's cottage at this point in her life.

Her grandmother was no longer living, and she missed their special bond and relationship. Her grandmother would know exactly what to say to make her feel better; she always knew when she was troubled or sad. She missed her so much. She was hoping that the cottage itself would fill in for her grandmother and offer her the solace that she desperately needed right now.

Peace and quiet . . . no rehearsals, no performances, no pain, no sorrow, no stress!

Her mother and grandmother had sacrificed everything for her dance lessons. Her grandmother was her cook, her chauffeur, her cheerleader, and her most precious promoter. Working countless hours had enabled Monique, Elizabeth's mother, to finance the lessons. She had carried their dreams with her over the years, and she was tired. She was tired of having the weight of performances on her shoulders. She was tired of always being the reliable and fully controlled prima ballerina. She needed a rest and a change of pace.

Elizabeth stared straight ahead so they wouldn't think she had seen anything and then sped away from the scene. She had driven for ten minutes when she saw a number of headlights coming up behind her. Her heart raced wildly. She thought for sure that the motorcycle gang members decided to remove any witnesses to their altercation. She increased her speed slightly. Her hands were trembling, and she was watching in the mirror as they quickly approached.

Much to her surprise, the motorcycles started passing her. She slowed a little to let the whole bunch of them pass. They did. They swerved around her car and kept on going down the road. She didn't know what to do. "Shit," she said. "Shit, shit." She knew that she could not keep going and ignore what she had seen. She did not want to stop, but she couldn't help herself.

I'm the one in the theatre always saying to myself, "Don't go back," and, "Don't go down the basement!" The killer is waiting for you! How stupid can you be? Why am I driving back? Away from the cottage where there is no one and only peace? I should have my head examined! I'll just drive by and take a peek, and then I'll be satisfied and on my way. Okay . . . it was close to here. I don't see anything. Oh there—there's a motorcycle on its side! It's only a motorcycle. They must've had the man on the back of one of those bikes that passed me. Okay, now you're satisfied . . . turn around and get on with it. Conscience appeased. Deep breath and turn the wheel. It's really late now.

"Shit."

Was that a hand? No . . . keep driving! Why did I pull over? My caution lights are flashing in my head! I'm sitting in the theatre thinking, Don't go there; the killer is waiting.

Having pulled over onto the shoulder, she continued looking in her rearview mirror. She reluctantly opened her door and started running back to the spot where she had seen a group of motorcyclists beating up a man. She saw a hand lying on the ground.

Oh Shit! It was a hand! Oh God! It's the man.

The man was twisted, with torn clothes, and lay on the ground in an unnatural position.

So much blood!

She had to check to see if he was alive. She couldn't turn her back on an injured person. If something as terrible as this happened to her, she certainly wouldn't want someone to just pass her by. She was sure the man was dead and hesitated on checking his pulse. The fear of returning motorcycles was making her think a mile a minute. But she couldn't turn around without checking. She had come this far and decided to continue.

Okay, I'll check his pulse, and if he's dead, I'll call the police and leave an anonymous message. There's nothing I can do for him . . . it's a motorcycle gang thing!

She didn't actually believe that; she was trying to convince herself to mind her own business and leave the man alone. She bent over and put her hand around his wrist. There was a pulse. He was still alive. Now she had to decide what to do. If she left him and called the police anonymously, she might not get any more involved. But what if he stopped breathing while she went to the cottage? There would be no one around to help him. She did know first aid and CPR. Her mother had insisted on her getting certified so that she could be prepared in case of an emergency. Her mother had been right. But if she stayed, her involvement might get back to the motorcycle gang, and she might be in danger. What should she do? She knew the second she had seen his hand that she could not leave this man alone in the dark on the side of a road. That's not the way she was raised; you helped people to the best of your ability. You did not abandon someone in their hour of need.

Shit!

Elizabeth did not realize that Michael was aware of someone touching him and leaning over him. He couldn't see because his eyes were swollen shut, but he could feel a soft hand wrapping itself around his wrist, even though the pain removed the softness of the touch. He couldn't think straight. All he felt was pain and the hand on his wrist. His instincts took over. He grabbed it.

Elizabeth jumped and screamed. "Jesus! Oh, my God!"

It felt like her heart was going to jump out of her throat. She stood staring at the body. His right hand had just grabbed hers and now lay across his shoulder. She was breathing hard and fast.

Shit! What do I do now?

"I have to do something," she said.

Her first-aid skills kicked in. As the instructor had told all the students, she had to reassure the injured party. She decided to reassure the man and tell him that she was going for help, that she was going to call the police and emergency assistance. She would cover him to keep him warm and then make her calls.

She knelt down on the ground and spoke softly into his ear.

"Hello, please don't grab me. I'm here to help you. You're really hurt. You shouldn't move. I'm going to get a blanket, and I'll call for help, and someone will come take care of you. I'm not going to hurt you. I just want to make sure that someone comes to help."

"No," whispered the man.

What was that? What did he say? Shit!

Elizabeth's brain was working a million miles per second. She couldn't believe that he had been able to talk.

Michael could not let her call the cops; too many questions to answer and too much attention. He had to convince this person not to call for help and to help him get away. *I have to get the hell out of here,* he thought. *If they come back and find out I'm alive, they'll finish me off for sure. And they'll kill her too.*

He knew all too well that the person, most likely a woman from the voice, would also be in danger. They would not want to leave any loose ends. They never left loose ends. They figured for sure that he would die on the side of the road. They both had to get out of there and fast. He had to convince her to get out *and* to take him with her. He had to muster up the strength to speak again. Every little movement caused a great deal of pain.

"No, please. No, please," Michael said with a gasp.

Elizabeth could not believe that he didn't want her to call for help.

"I'm sorry, sir. You're really hurt badly. You're bleeding everywhere, and I'm afraid that those people are going to come back and find me here and find you here. I have to get help. You might die if I don't get you some help!"

"No help! No help!" Michael could barely get the words out.

What do you mean—no help? Are you crazy!

"Sir, you really need help! I'm going to call the police, and everything will be okay. The more time we take here, the worse it is for you."

"No police. They'll kill me and you!"

She knew he was going to say that even before she heard it. She had a strange feeling that the motorcycle gang would come back to make sure they had killed him.

"Help me up!" said Michael.

Elizabeth ran back to her car and grabbed a blanket out of the trunk. She put the blanket down on the ground and rolled Michael's bruised body onto it. He moaned. She knew it was causing him a great deal of pain, but it was the only way she could think of to get him into her car. She couldn't believe what she was doing. This was not typical first-aid procedure. She had always followed procedures. She was doing something completely foreign to her, but she felt that it was right. "Follow your heart," her grandmother used to say. Well, it may have felt right, but she knew that there was danger involved. She dragged the blanket and Michael back to her car.

"I don't know how you made it to my car! Please don't move too much. You're causing more bleeding! Oh God! Let's get you down in the backseat."

Elizabeth was lean and long, but she was very strong. Michael could not help her at all. He was in so much pain that he had given into it and given into her.

He moaned when she lay him down. The pain went through his back like a knife. Had there been a knife? He couldn't remember. It didn't matter now. He was at the mercy of this woman. He knew he had to keep still or he'd bleed out. The backseat felt good. The blanket felt good. He felt his body go off to sleep.

"Hello, are you okay? Are you comfortable?" Elizabeth asked in a panic.

She realized that he was now unconscious. She hoped she had not done anything wrong. She checked his pulse. She thanked God that there was still a pulse, but it was very slow. This bruised man had lost a lot of blood. She had to get away from the scene as fast as possible. Just as she was getting into her car, her eyes caught something shining in the moonlight. It was the chrome on the motorcycle! She started thinking quickly again. She decided that the motorcycle had to be moved or covered up or both. People, or maybe the police, seeing it lying on its side, would stop to see if there was anyone hurt. They would start looking for the driver, and then they would see the blood. Then they would start an investigation. Her car might leave some kind of sign that she was involved. She had to make sure there was no way to trace anything back to her.

She ran back to the motorcycle. It took all her strength to get it up on its wheels and push it. She pushed it down the embankment and let it crash again. She covered it with as many branches as she could. She did a thorough job. Kicking her feet around the dirt to spread it out and cover up the blood took precious time. But she thought it was well worth it. She couldn't believe that she was doing this, any of it! But she was trusting her heart and not listening to her brain. She knew she might regret this decision, but she followed through, as usual.

My heart cannot beat any faster than it's beating now. I have performed the longest dance and never had so much trouble breathing! These stupid branches are scratching my hands and arms everywhere. Shut up and hurry up before someone comes!

From the road, you couldn't see the motorcycle.

Maybe I'll come back in the daylight to check if you can see it. Get the hell out!

She turned her head and saw a landmark. *Lightning tree!* There was a tree that had been struck by lightning on the other side of the road. It was a tall white birch tree, and it had been split in two. That became her landmark for where she had covered the motorcycle.

She finished kicking the dirt to cover the blood and her tire tracks. She had seen those *CSI* shows on TV.

They can find you through your tire tracks! Oh yeah, now I'm a forensic expert!

When she got to her car, her heart was racing. She was used to tension and anxiety. Her brain was functioning at lightning speed now—just the way she liked it. She pushed the odometer on her car so that she could know the distance from the cottage to the spot for her return inspection. She figured that she would have to come back for some reason or another. She shook her head. There were no sounds from the backseat. She hoped he would still be alive by the time they arrived at the cottage.

Chapter 2

May 3, 2004

Michael Ryan. That was the name on the driver's license she found in the pocket of his jeans. His wallet had been soaked in blood, so she rinsed everything off and laid it out to dry. At least she knew his name.

Can someone stay asleep for one week and still recover?

It had been a long week for Elizabeth. She had not thought of herself once. She had not enjoyed the tranquility of her grandmother's old cottage—the silence, the sound of water lapping onto the shore, the sound of crickets and frogs. She was focused on Michael Ryan. He had not woken up since she pulled him out of her car and dragged him into the cottage on a blanket. She didn't know what to do; she just did what her heart told her.

Elizabeth, for some reason not even logical to her, had decided to help this injured man. She made up her mind to believe that he was unjustifiably beaten up. She had sensed that this was not a fair encounter; so many men against one human being. Had it been a fair fight, one man would have been fighting one man. She was always a supporter of the underdog, and Michael Ryan seemed to be the underdog.

She did as he had asked. She did not contact the police, which maybe she should have. But she followed her instinct and decided to support Michael Ryan.

She had driven west into a little town and stocked up on first-aid supplies and food. She had been trickling water in his mouth in hopes of keeping him alive. She dropped Pedialyte into his mouth to replace the electrolyte loss. He, most likely, should have been hospitalized, but Elizabeth was afraid that the men who had beaten him up would be able to track him down. So she decided to do it on her own and prayed that she had made the right decision.

She had removed all his clothes and washed his entire body, marveling at his muscular built. He had a trim, fit physique. There were many scars though—and now many wounds to heal. So many bruises! They had beaten almost every inch of his body. It was swollen and every color of the rainbow. She had washed his face and shaven off his beard. Keeping the wounds disinfected was her number-one concern. He had a nice face with a strong jaw line. She couldn't see his eyes because they were still swollen shut.

Elizabeth treated her unfortunate stranger with dignity and care. She knew to move his body as little as possible to lessen further injury, especially his eyes. Elizabeth bathed his eyes with water and applied cold compresses to help reduce the swelling. Gentle and caring strokes were her plan. She had suffered many injuries while dancing and had learned how to treat bruising, abrasions, and muscle damage. Patience and sensitive care was needed. And that is what Elizabeth was ready to give. Worry plagued her.

Would he be able to see?

She washed all of his clothes, but the stains would not come out. So she burned them all. When she had gone into town, she had bought a shirt and a pair of pants, some socks, and a pair of boxer shorts. She smiled when she bought those because she didn't know if he was a briefs man or a boxer shorts man. He hadn't been wearing any underwear! She thought he would look great in boxer shorts, so boxer shorts it was.

July 2004

That's all she put on him, so that his wounds would heal. Six weeks had passed. It was July, and it was hot, so boxer shorts and thin gauze was all that covered his beaten body. He was in her grandmother's bed, and she slept on the floor in case he woke up in the middle of the night.

She had done that as a child. Snuck downstairs into her grandmother's bedroom with her blanket and curled up on the floor, afraid of the lightning and thunder outside, feeling secure beside her Gram. That was a great feeling. She had not had that feeling of security since they had stopped coming to the cottage so many years ago. She longed for that. She did feel secure that Michael was being looked after by her grandmother's spirit. He was in her bedroom and enveloped by her arms in her bed. Elizabeth was resolute that he would recover.

Michael Ryan looked peaceful on the bed, body laid out straight with gauze all over his wounds, and the smell of disinfectant everywhere in the cottage. But Elizabeth was afraid. Was she qualified to take care of him properly? Just from her experience with an injured and abused body? Faith, belief, and instinct were carrying her through the days. Internal bleeding was a danger, but she had managed to get nutrients into his body. She had one huge concern. He wasn't waking up. Why wasn't he waking up?

Elizabeth was diligent in this rescue. She took on the duties as she did her dance. She persevered through doubts and pain. For some reason, covering her tracks on the road and in town was paramount.

The motorcycle was completely covered with branches now. She had returned the next day, at breakneck speed, to check out the scene by the lightning tree. The odometer signaled the location of the beating. There were little glimpses of the motorcycle, only because she knew where to look. After she was finished covering it some more, no one could tell that there was a bloodied motorcycle hidden in the trees. She had been so afraid of a driver, or worse yet, a motorcycle, passing by that she had moved as quickly and efficiently as possible. She kicked the dirt around even more. She picked up a few things strewn around, even a knife she knew had entered Michael Ryan's body a few times. Now her prints were on it! She had tied a rock to it, brought it out on the lake, and let it drop to the bottom of the lake—the serene lake, the lake she had always loved. The lake now held her secret.

It had been therapeutic for her not to think of dancing, not to think of letting down her dance troupe, not to think of how angry her manager would be, not to think of how disappointed everyone would be in the lead dancer leaving in the middle of the ballet season, and not to think of Peter. The ballet was a great success. She had been receiving the greatest of reviews for her performances. She was the talk of the ballet world. This was what she had worked for and had dreamed of her entire life, being the prima ballerina of a successful ballet. But she was not happy. Something was missing, and she had to find it! Her grandmother had told her on her deathbed to be happy and to follow her heart.

For the past weeks, she had not thought about her heart or dancing. She bathed, cleansed, and wrapped Michael Ryan's wounds. She patted his face and trickled more water down his throat to keep him hydrated. There was no dancing. She had not worked out or stretched. She was focused on this man in her grandmother's bed. She was pleading that he would wake up and talk to her and tell her if it hurt and if she was doing things properly.

No one knows Michael Ryan is here, and no one knows I'm here. So, I'm safe.

She sat on her grandmother's rocking chair, staring at Michael Ryan and praying that something would move— to show her that she hadn't killed him after all! It was a beautiful day, again. Water was hitting the shore just outside the kitchen door. Slight breezes were cooling things off a little, but it was still July and still hot. For some reason, she was beginning to relax in a strange way. The cottage was starting to heal her wounds as well as Michael's wounds.

She could close her eyes and go back twenty years and hear her mother and grandmother talking and laughing. She could remember the smell of the cooking and the smell of both women, smells she would never forget. This place still made her feel warm inside, despite all that had happened in the last few weeks. The cottage had been a Godsend! Believing Michael Ryan would survive was encouraging her. There were angels guarding him.

Unbeknownst to Elizabeth, Michael was starting to return to life. He couldn't move, but he could hear and smell. He smelled fresh flowers, and he could hear a creaking sound. He wasn't sure what was making that sound. He decided to try to say something, even though his throat felt like sandpaper.

"Hello."

Elizabeth jumped up from the floor. She thought she heard him speak. She turned on the light. *Did I hear something?*

What the hell was that? Michael thought. *Someone turned on a light, but I still can't see. But I see light. Okay, let's try again.*

"Hello?"

"Hello," repeated Elizabeth. "Hello, yes, yes, I hear you. Please don't move too much. You're very hurt. Your eyes are swollen; that's why you can't see. Wait, I'll get you a little water."

Elizabeth ran to the fridge to get some water and poured just a little into his mouth. He swallowed.

Yes, he thought.

"I'm sure that's a little better now. I'll give you a little more water in a few minutes . . . a little at a time. My name is Elizabeth, and you're at my cottage in a bed. No one knows you're here. I didn't call the police, like you asked me. I haven't told anyone, but I'm very worried about you. You were badly beaten, and your eyes are still a little swollen. Maybe I can bathe them again and get the swelling down a little. Here's a little water again. I hope I'm not hurting you."

She was rambling, but the adrenaline was running through her.

"I know that your name is Michael Ryan. I'm afraid I had to burn your clothes, as the blood stains would not come out. I've dried out your identification and wallet, and all is okay."

"How?"

That came out clearly. Michael couldn't believe what he was hearing. People had not been supportive as he grew up. He was suspicious about what he was hearing.

"Oh, I picked you up from the side of the road after the bikers left you, and you asked me not to call the police, and then you passed out. I took you to my family cottage, and you've been asleep for weeks now. Your body has to heal. You should try to keep still. Here's a little more water."

Trying her best to convince him that her sentiments were real and honest, Elizabeth continued to talk and make him comfortable. She propped Michael's head up a little more. She felt it safer to move him since he actually spoke a word. He swallowed the water a little more easily. *That's good,* she thought. *He needs the water in his body.* She laid his head back down.

With that, Michael moaned.

"I'm so sorry. You must be in a lot of pain. I have some liquid painkiller here, and I'll give you some if you'd like."

"Yes."

Saying that hurt so much Mike could not believe it. *Why does talking hurt?* he thought. *Drugs, yes drugs, give me drugs!*

Elizabeth got up, went to the medicine cabinet, and got out the liquid painkiller she bought in the town drugstore. She put some medicine on a spoon and slowly lifted Michael's head and poured it into his mouth, hoping he could swallow it. He swallowed it fine and then frowned. Elizabeth knew that the medicine had gone down his throat properly and smiled a little at the reaction to the taste of the medicine. Any reaction was better than watching him lay lifeless.

Elizabeth lowered Michael's head back onto the bed and returned the medicine to the cabinet. Sitting on the edge of the bed very carefully, she looked at this broken man and wondered what she could do to help him even more, imagining the excruciating pain. She got up, got a basin, water, and a cloth, and began wiping his face. It was hot, and he was sweating. She patted his shoulders, arms, and hands, his legs and feet.

There, she thought. *That should be a little better.*

Mike had never had anyone bathe him. He couldn't say that he didn't like it because it felt so good. She was wiping away the heat and bringing some feeling to his skin. He knew he was alive because he could feel every inch she touched.

Who is this woman? Why is she doing this?

He fell back asleep thinking about the woman, the bathing, and the pain.

Elizabeth returned the basin and cloth and lay back down on the floor beside the bed. He had fallen asleep. She could tell by his heavy breathing. It was a calming sound now. He was alive if he was breathing heavily! She fell asleep thinking about the man, the breathing, and his pain.

The sun shone into the window directly onto Elizabeth's face, waking her up. It was a beautiful clear morning. She got up and started up the kettle for a cup of coffee. Looking out the window, she could see clear across the lake. It was so calm that it looked like a blue mirror. She loved that time of day. Birds singing and water lapping onto the shore were the normal sounds of this cottage. She turned and looked at Michael Ryan on the bed. He was still sleeping.

Good! She could enjoy her coffee.

She sat on the Adirondack chair with her feet up on the ottoman her grandmother made. It was looking a little ratty now, but she loved it. She remembered watching her grandmother finish her little project of the day and the smile on her face when she finished. She was pleased with the results, and so were Elizabeth and her mother.

Sweet times.

While she gazed out at the calm lake, she told herself that coffee tasted much better at the cottage. Her mind wandered to the city—to the ballet world.

I wonder how the performances are going. I hope it didn't hurt too many people, when I left so suddenly.

Peter would have been disappointed and hurt. Making this selfish decision was something that had to be done. She had to take care of herself for a change. She had no personal life—only ballet. She didn't have friends outside of the ballet world. Maria, her best friend, was a friend since they were three in their first dance class. She trained and worked and trained and worked. She had been doing this for so long that she forgot how to smile, how to laugh, and how to love. Suffocation was occurring. Planning her escape had taken her only a few weeks.

I can't think about that right now. I have to get up, get some clean water, and bathe Mr. Michael Ryan back to health. No time to think about what brought me here. I have to think about what I'm doing here. Yes, concentrate on Mr. Ryan.

Elizabeth got up quickly from her peaceful sitting place and headed for the kitchen. She took a peek at Michael and thought that maybe he was awake. She got the basin, water, and cloth again.

"Good morning. Are you awake?"

A little nod of the head.

"You nodded! That's great! I'll just get you a little water and maybe start some soup later. How's that?"

Elizabeth got the water quickly, gently raised Michael's head, and slowly poured the water into his mouth.

Swallowing was easier this time. Her hands were so soft on his head, he could hardly feel them. The water was great. He felt it slowly trickling down his throat, giving life to his body. Now she was bathing him again. Damn that felt good on his face!

She's wiping my eyes . . . Jesus, that hurts!

"I hope I'm not hurting you too much. I thought I'd give your eyes an extra little wash to see if you could start opening them. I know it must be scary and frustrating not to see. Shall I continue?"

Again, a little nod of the head.

"Good," she said. She was afraid of hurting him further. She knew about pain. She had danced through pain and in spite of pain. So she understood his reactions. She was particularly worried about his eyes. Having someone's hands all over your body was a vulnerable position for anyone.

"I hope you don't mind me touching you so much." She chuckled a little. "I guess you don't have much of a choice right now. I'm kind of taking over here! That's new to me! But this should help you feel fresh for the day."

Elizabeth got up and returned the basin and cloth to the kitchen. She would bathe Michael every half hour to make sure he wasn't too hot and a little more comfortable.

Michael Ryan could not believe what was happening. This woman was bathing him over and over again. It was a lifeline for him. All her movements and touching were soft and gentle. He could feel the caring in every wipe.

Why would someone care for someone she does not know? he thought. *That's crazy! Maybe there's a reason behind her actions. That's probably it,* he thought. *She thinks she's gonna get something out of this. Why else would someone bathe another person over and over again? Sorry, lady, I've got nothing to give!*

Chapter 3

July 2004

Five days of bathing and still his eyes had not opened. He was afraid to think about not being able to see again. His body was not hurting as much now. He could sit up with a little help. He could actually eat a little bit of soft food. He could feel his strength returning, feel life returning to his body. Working out, lifting weights, and running had been part of his normal day. He did not like being so still and incapacitated now. This was the longest he had gone without working out. He missed it, but he had to heal.

On the sixth morning after becoming conscious, Elizabeth woke up with a burning desire to dance. Needing to feel those movements and pains again, she decided to do some movements and stretches using the railing of the deck. If the music was soft, and she stood in front of the window to stretch, she could still keep an eye on Michael. He was having a nap after breakfast. She changed into a white ballet leotard. Her skin was so pale. She had not sat out in the sun at all. She was still the ballet white she was weeks ago. She tied her pale blonde hair into a ponytail. Her thin, blonde hair was down to her shoulder blades, the perfect length to make a ballet bun. She had beautiful, long, thin, fairly muscular legs. Her arms were long and sinewy, and her fingers were long and thin, perfect to demonstrate the perfect ballet moves. She felt good and ready to dance! She was excited, and her heart raced.

I'll put on some Beethoven, she thought. *I love the pace of his movements. I'll just feel the music and stretch. Oh, this will be fun!*

She took a quick look at Michael Ryan and set up her workout session. He was still sleeping. He was doing so much better. Feeling a little proud of herself and how she had dealt with the situation, she realized that the situation could have ended in disaster. He had been very hurt, and she had taken a big chance in dealing with his injuries on her own. It was time for her to spend some time on herself.

The music started. She assumed her position beside the railing. Her hand rested on the railing with confidence and strength. Up went her left arm, and straight went her back. Her chin was raised just at that perfect angle, and the dance began!

Mike heard some soft music playing—not his cup of tea! But it was soothing, he thought, so he sat up to feel a little more breeze coming through the window. He decided to try to open his eyes.

Maybe if I go slow and concentrate, I'll be able to finally open these stupid eyes! I'm sick and tired of feeling like an invalid here.

Plus, he could feel that something kept on moving in the light in front of him.

What's moving?

It seemed that his eyes were glued together. He reached to his right and got the cloth out of the water and wiped his eyes, over and over again.

Hey, I feel some movement. Christ, please let this work. Go slowly, Mikey, old boy, otherwise you can hurt something. What is that moving in front of me? Damn I hate this shit! Okay, slow!

Mike's eyelids started to separate. The light hurt at first. His eyes hadn't been open for weeks.

Damn, that's bright!

Stubborn was a word that could be used to describe Michael Ryan, and this situation was not very different. Struggling through the pain, he actually got his eyes half-open and started to focus on the movement in front of him. He started to make out the cottage, the bed, his body wearing boxer shorts, his legs, the tables beside the bed, the window, and then he saw her! His heart just about stopped beating.

He saw a beautiful woman immersed in the music. Her body was moving like a swan through water. He couldn't believe his eyes and felt that he had never seen anything so moving in his life. She looked completely at ease and relaxed. He marveled at her beautiful and fine hair and her flawless skin. He swallowed hard and wondered why there was a knot in his stomach. He ignored that feeling.

What a sight to see after having my eyes closed for so long, he thought.

He must have sat there for fifteen minutes just watching Elizabeth move effortlessly in the breeze. She moved slowly to the music, and it seemed that she was feeling every note of the piano. She reached for the sky and down to the floor. She stretched forward, backward, and sideways.

Elizabeth was in her glory.

Wow, this feels great! How I love this piece! The old body can still move. But I'm going to feel this tomorrow, she thought. *Ha, I'll even enjoy that again. Yes, I have to focus on myself. Myself! Check on him. You forgot about him.*

Elizabeth turned to check on Michael Ryan in the bed. She stopped moving and stared wide-eyed. There, sitting in the bed, was Michael Ryan looking at her, with his eyes open. They were both wide-eyed and had their mouths open in shock. They both swallowed hard at the same time.

Jesus, her eyes are so green I can see the color from here. Have I ever seen anyone more beautiful? Stop thinking like this. Get yourself together here. What the hell is wrong with you?

His eyes . . . they're blue. They're so blue.

She could barely see the color as his eyes were only half-open, but she could see the cobalt blue eyes peeking out from the slits.

Elizabeth was the first to break the stare. She smiled.

Jesus, how to light up the freaking world!

She broke her posture, turned the music off, grabbed her towel, and went to the kitchen door to greet Michael Ryan's eyes.

She's coming! Jesus, she moves like an angel.

"I can't believe you've opened your eyes."

"Yeah, it took a little effort, but I figured it was worth a try."

"I don't think you should experience so much light."

She got up and closed the curtains. The light now was soft and not so bright. It did feel better to Mike.

"Thanks," he said.

"You have to take a little light at a time. How long have you had them open?"

"I just opened them when you looked at me," he said. "Perfect timing!"

"Yes, it was. And I'm so glad for you. Now, you lay back, and I'll just wash them a little. I'm sure they're tired already!"

Yeah, that was a good idea, he thought. *I do feel tired.*

He lay back, and she quickly picked up the basin and got some fresh water and a fresh cloth. She applied soft strokes across his eyelids and gentle moves around his face.

I can't believe how good that feels. She barely touches my skin. Okay, enough of that. Focus on getting the hell out of here!

Elizabeth set a cold compress to soothe his eyes.

It was quite a happy evening for both of them. Mike could open his eyes enough to feed himself for the first time in weeks. He ate more food than he had in days. Elizabeth laughed at the amount of food he consumed. She wasn't a great cook, but her grandmother had taught her the basics. She had made a chicken stew with some fresh vegetables. She used the herbs that grew around the cottage.

Her grandmother had planted those herbs. It made the meal that much more special to Elizabeth. Her mother had never been a really good cook! She tried, but couldn't cut it. Elizabeth had inherited the cooking genes from Gram! *This was a Gram stew,* she thought.

Mike could not believe how good the stew tasted. *It might be because I haven't eaten much of anything for a while, but shit, this is good!*

"I can't move! I think I over ate! It was really good. Thanks."

"You're welcome," she said. "I'm happy you enjoyed my attempt at cooking."

She picked up his tray and cleaned up the dishes. There was extra stew for tomorrow's lunch, and she put that in the fridge.

She turned to look at Michael Ryan. He had lain back down against the soft pillows and was staring out the window, watching the clouds going by. The scent of flowers, the blue skies, the soft clouds, and the slight breeze made it a beautiful July day.

He's getting his strength back, she thought. *That's good!* She noticed his strong chin and the edges on his cheeks. *Nice-looking guy underneath all that hair! Oh, what are you thinking about? This guy is as far away from your world as an alien. Enough of that!*

She sat in the rocking chair on the left side of the bed and joined Mike watching the clouds. They did this in comfortable silence for at least one hour, and then Elizabeth noticed that Michael Ryan had dozed off. She took the opportunity to walk down the steps, across the deck, and to the end of the wharf. She sat on the Adirondack chair, listened to the sounds of the lake, and watched the sun set.

This is peace. I love this place.

When darkness started to arrive, Elizabeth got up and started back to the cottage. It was time to bathe Michael Ryan and get ready for bed.

She's coming back. Funny how this place doesn't feel the same when she's not in it.

"Hello, all set to get ready for bed? I'll just get the basin and cloth."

"I think maybe I can sit here and do it myself now, if you don't mind."

"No, not at all. Just let me know if you need help."

Mike managed to get things done, but with a lot of pain (he kept his mouth shut) and a lot of time. Still, he felt that he had made significant progress. The next thing that happened, he really didn't expect. Elizabeth got out the little cot, laid it on the floor, got her duvet and pillow, and started lowering herself to the floor.

"What the hell are you doing?"

His tone of voice startled her.

"I'm just going to lie here, as I've done for the past weeks, just in case you need help in the middle of the night."

"There must be another bedroom in this place . . ."

"Yes, of course there is. My normal room is in the loft—next to a washroom and my mummy's room, actually."

"Well, then you should actually be sleeping in it. I'm not going to sleep in a bed and have a woman sleep on the floor! No way!"

"I don't mind."

"I do. I do very much. I'm awake now. If I need help, I'll call you. I promise. I can also do things for myself now. I'm not going to fall apart. And you, young lady, need a good night sleep in a bed! Your own bed, it looks like!"

Elizabeth stood staring at Michael Ryan, trying to figure out why he was saying what he was saying. She worried that if he did too much too soon, he could possibly reinjure himself.

"I'm worried!"

"Don't be. This is the way it is going to be!"

"Yes, sir. Well, I'll leave you to your first night alone then. I'll pick up my linens and be off! It will be nice to sleep in my old bed. Goodnight, Michael."

Michael. That's the first time I heard her say my name. I don't like Michael, but I like the way it sounds coming from her.

"Goodnight," he replied.

Her room had not changed since she was a teenager. The sheets were still pink and green. Her old iron bed with brass ends was still standing. Her dresser was covered in green and yellow daisies. Why had nothing changed in years? The stuffed animals were still all over her room. She still loved them!

Such a warm feeling, she thought. *So many great nights spent here, looking out that window at the lake and listening to the sounds.* Her mother and Gram used to sit on the deck talking and laughing until Elizabeth fell asleep. Gram was always awake in the morning with breakfast waiting.

And now, Michael Ryan was in Gram's bed. It was strange to be lying in her bed at the cottage without her grandmother there. It was even stranger to have a mysterious man in the cottage. Elizabeth was relieved that her decision to help Michael and not call the police or take him to a hospital had proven to be okay. It did not seem, at this point, that she had harmed Michael Ryan with her care. Still, it was difficult to fall asleep. She was worried that Michael would need some help and that she wouldn't hear him. But her bed did feel good.

Chapter 4

Elizabeth's mother was not a morning person. When they were at the cottage, she hardly ever got out of bed before noon. At home, she dragged herself out of bed every morning to get to her job at the magazine. Monique Hamilton was the fashion editor at *Vogue* magazine. She loved her job. She had worked her way up from the typing pool many years before. She watched every move made by the executives. She knew their likes and dislikes, and she made sure that when she was around, their likes were up and center. And they fell for it! She was promoted from the typing pool. After that first promotion, she was on her way. Her second favorite position had been as a buyer of fashion. She got to choose the clothes and designers to feature each month. She learned a lot about the fashion business, very quickly. She became assistant editor, and when the editor died of a heart attack, Monique became the new fashion editor. She had secured a position guaranteeing the future for herself and her daughter.

Elizabeth was the center of Monique's world. She was focused on her career and loved her job, but she received all her joys and accomplished all her dreams through Elizabeth. Elizabeth, her beautiful blonde daughter who had been "an accident" of a one-night stand. Her father didn't even know that she existed, mostly because Monique didn't remember whom she had slept with that fateful night. She had never regretted continuing with her pregnancy. She was delighted with her beautiful, tiny, blonde-haired daughter. She was perfect. She was bright, polite, and loved being with her mother. This gave Monique so much joy. Even her mother, Elizabeth's grandmother, was forever happy that Elizabeth came into their world.

They were strong women. Monique had learned how to be strong from her mother. Her father had died when she was very young, and her mother had raised her, working two jobs to have enough money to give her daughter a good education. Monique appreciated her hard work and had, herself, worked hard. The Hamilton women deserved what they had.

Monique registered Elizabeth for ballet lessons when she was three. Her mother would take her to the dance studio twice a week after school. The three would meet for dinner after each lesson. It became a tradition.

By the age of seven, it became apparent that Elizabeth was not just a normal little girl taking ballet lessons. She was now attending ballet classes four times per week and practicing at home in between. They had moved to an apartment with four bedrooms so that one room could be renovated into a small ballet studio. They had installed ballet bars and mirrors so that Elizabeth could dance whenever she felt the urge. The ballet world was starting to notice the beautiful, ethereal blonde from the East End Ballet

School! Monique received many offers from ballet schools with large incentives for Elizabeth. But Elizabeth wanted to dance where she felt at home—with her instructor, Mademoiselle Fleming!

Mademoiselle Fleming was Elizabeth's second mother. She instilled in Elizabeth a desire to reach for the stars and the ethic of hard work. Mademoiselle had never reached the level of success she knew was in the future for Elizabeth. She loved watching the girl dance. Everyone that watched Elizabeth dance could see how much she loved it, how she felt every note of the music. And she practiced, and she practiced in their little studio in the East End of New York City. She did not want to dance anywhere else.

When Elizabeth was twelve, Mademoiselle had to make a difficult choice. She knew many people were approaching Monique about Elizabeth's ballet future. She decided to do some investigating into the various schools. She made a list of the pros and cons of all the schools. She assessed the instructors and the type of instruction instituted at the schools. When she felt she had all the information needed to make the best decision for Elizabeth, she brought it all to Monique. Mademoiselle knew she would lose her star dancer one day, and she wanted to make sure that the decision would be for Elizabeth's best interest and not a dancing school's best interest. It was time to make a move, just before Elizabeth went into high school.

After many hours of discussion and many phone calls from various school directors, Mademoiselle, Monique, and Gram had narrowed it down to two schools. The National

Conservatory of Ballet of New York was one of the choices, and the other was a school that required Elizabeth to become a boarded student—the Julliard School of Dance. Both were offering Elizabeth full scholarships, and both schools were eager to get Elizabeth as a student. It was now time for the women in Elizabeth's life to present their findings to her and to help Elizabeth make a very important decision.

Elizabeth was not happy. She did not want to leave the East End Ballet School. She wanted to continue studying under Mademoiselle Fleming. It took many, many talks for Mademoiselle to convince Elizabeth that it was time for her to experience different instructors and different styles of dance. "It is time for you to develop your skills with different instructors," Mademoiselle urged.

"I don't need to develop. You're the best teacher in the world. I want to stay with you. Why would I want to leave?"

"You're not leaving. You're just moving on to another stage."

"No. I don't want to move on."

"You must. God has given you the gift of dance. You must nourish that gift. So many new experiences. I cannot deny you that education and experience."

"Please, please don't make me go to those places. They don't know me like you do."

"And it is because I know you that I'm telling you to go out and soar like you can. You must promise me that you will always work hard and always, always dance with a smile."

It was obvious that Mademoiselle was not going to back down. Elizabeth had to have faith in her opinion. She reluctantly agreed to visit the two schools.

It was August, and the city was hot. It was even hotter inside the two ballet schools. Dancers walked around everywhere. Studios were being used at all times. Music could be heard coming from many directions. Elizabeth loved this atmosphere. It was exciting and incited a desire to dance within her. But she kept very quiet and poker faced while listening to the pitch of the school directors. She did not want to live away from home—no way! She could not imagine being away from her mother and Gram.

Then she walked into Eva Gutcher's studio. They quietly entered the studio just as Eva was trying to get her class to feel a certain lift in the music. At that lift, she wanted them to raise both arms and let the music lift them off the floor in a perfect pirouette. They were not getting the timing. Eva was hitting the floor with her walking stick in the cadence of the music and then slammed it on the floor when the dancers were to lift up. She tried over and over to get them to listen closely to the music. She even demonstrated the motion of the lift herself. She could still dance, even at fifty-five. *Bang, bang, bang,* she repeated with her stick.

In the corner of her eye, Eva could see this waif of a girl swaying to the music and closing her eyes. She noticed that at the precise time when the dancers should be lifting, this tiny girl would straighten her back, and her shoulders would pop upward. Then the girl would smile as if she understood what the musician had wanted the listener to feel.

She tried one more time to have her class get the timing in the choreography—to no avail. As she spoke, she walked toward the young girl, grabbed her hand, and said, "Play the music again please, and this young lady will show us exactly what I mean."

Elizabeth was startled when the woman took her hand and moved her onto the middle of the dance floor, but when the music started, all inhibitions disappeared. Elizabeth danced, and at the precise lift in the music, Elizabeth left the ground, pirouetted in the air, and landed on one foot with both hands still reaching for the stars. The room became silent.

"Thank you," said Eva.

"You're welcome," said Elizabeth, "and thank you."

The instructor looked at the student and at that moment, the deal was struck! Elizabeth would become a ballet student at the Julliard School of Dance, and she would be in boarding school. Academic and ballet instruction would occur every day but Sunday. School began at 8:00 a.m., and classes finished at 7:00 p.m. Everyone was expected to complete their homework from 7:00 to 9:00 p.m., and then lights out. Elizabeth loved it! She didn't like not being home except for Sundays, but she absorbed every word from every instructor and teacher.

Eva had never seen such a dedicated dancer. They developed a special relationship that would continue until Eva's death!

Chapter 5

July 2004

After finally falling asleep, Elizabeth had the best sleep she had had in years. She had sweet dreams of dancing, and her mother and grandmother were sitting in the audience watching and smiling.

Mike, on the other hand, could not settle down. He wondered what she was doing upstairs. He was too weak to go up the stairs. He hadn't even walked yet. He decided that tomorrow he would try to get up and see if he could move his gimpy legs.

What the hell am I going to do? I'm going to have to figure out what to do next and where to go from here. It's obvious that I can't go back to life as it was. I'm going to have to make decisions here and quickly.

Before March 2004

The hand life had dealt Mike had not been great. He was a disillusioned member of a bike gang. He was a twenty-eight-year-old who had never grown up, who had never held a full-time job, who had no family ties, and who didn't give a damn about anyone but himself. He had nothing to show for his time on earth and had proven no importance to anyone! He had not figured out why he existed and didn't really care. Mike's problems began when he did start caring. He had never killed anyone. He had been involved in many fights, but he rationalized those as being defensive, having to protect himself. He hadn't raped anyone, although he pretended that he had. He had robbed and stolen, but he had never been caught. He had a clear police record, unbelievable after eleven years of living the biker lifestyle. But the lifestyle had started to lose its shine with Mike. It wasn't fun anymore, and he didn't know why. He couldn't put his finger on it. He just was very unsettled.

Mike's drunkard of a father died when Mike was seventeen. His mother had passed away when Mike was just a toddler, so there were no memories of her except for one soft song, "Beautiful, Beautiful Blue Eyes." That was the extent of his family memories. He had tried to forget his past—the drinking, the beatings, the verbal and emotional abuse. He still frowned when he thought about him.

After his father died, Mike lived on the street hustling for money to eat. One day, he defended a guy on a motorcycle who was being outnumbered by a group of men obviously from a rival gang. Mike knew he shouldn't get involved, but the guy was going to get the crap beaten out of him. Well, they both got the crap beaten out of them, but the other guys looked worse. The man he helped was Big Al. To thank Mike, Big Al put him on the back of his Harley and took him to one of their biker houses. Mike had a roof over his head for the first time in six months. He could take a shower, and there were women . . . willing women. He thought he had hit the jackpot. Big Al was one of the leaders in their small group and grateful for Mike's help. He offered Mike a place to hang his hat, have some food, and have some sex. Mike could not resist.

Michael Ryan was a natural with a motorcycle. He quickly learned how to drive and maneuver one of the big bikes. Being at the right place at the right time, he inherited a fairly new bike when another biker was killed during a retaliation raid. That had scared the crap out of Mike. He had run for cover in the woods surrounding the house, and after twenty minutes of gunfire, three people lay dead, and everyone seemed just to think that was normal. So, he did too.

He had to prove himself to the others by robbing a few stores. He was also to rape a few girls to solidify his position in the gang. He made the girl promise to say that she was raped and to report it to the police. He could not and would not have sex with a woman that did not want to have sex. He was also certain that he would never kill another person, unless his life was in danger. He did not have that killer instinct that most of the gang members had, especially Big Al. Big Al had a long list of victims—robbery, rape, and murder—and he was proud of it. He thought Mike looked up to him for his great record. He didn't know that, in reality, Mike was afraid of Big Al.

Mike had started feeling that Big Al sensed a change in him.

There's gotta be more than this. That thought had popped into Mike's brain way too many times. *What the hell is going on?*

Then Big Al picked the last and final test for Mike. He had to take out the leader of a rival bike gang. Their group, Mid Town Boys, was having trouble with another biker group moving into their territory. He had never seen Mike kill anyone, and that started to bother Big Al. You had to prove yourself. You had to belong heart and soul in an organization for the organization to provide you with support and lodgings. Big Al felt that Mike had to prove his worth. The Hispanic bikers, Los Alamos, had started to invade their territory and were making ground, and it was time to teach them a lesson. It was time they realized who was in charge around here, the Mid Town Boys—namely, Big Al. It was time. And who better to carry out the job than his protégé, Mike Ryan.

"You know, Mike," said Big Al, "it's time to teach Los Alamos a lesson."

Mike nodded. He thought, *Here we go again. Al is gonna ride in on his white horse (his Harley) and go on another shooting spree and show that he's the leader of the pack again.* Mike had no idea that this time it was expected that he would be the one going on the shooting spree. But it was not a spree; it was only going to be one man, Jose Vega, the leader of Los Alamos. Big Al thought it would make a strong statement to the Hispanic bikers that this was MTB territory.

"So you agree?" questioned Big Al.

"Yup, all the way with you, big guy," said Mike.

"I'm glad to hear that," said Big Al. "Because you're the one that's gonna carry it out."

"What?" asked Mike.

"Yeah, you. It's time you show everyone that you're a threat to be reckoned with around here. You have to put the fear of God into everyone. This way you'll earn respect, and people will make sure they don't cross you. And what better way?"

Mike's stomach started to turn. How in the hell would he be able to kill another human being? What the hell was he going to do now? How could he pull this off? The pretend rapes were easy. He just paid off the girls and told them if they opened their mouths, he would come by and definitely rape them. That had worked so far. *Damn. Now what?*

"No better way, buddy," said Mike.

"That's the ticket. So you think about this tonight. And so will I. What would be the best way to get rid of this guy, and what would make the biggest statement? We want to scare the crap out of the other members of Los Alamos. We want them to be afraid, very afraid, of the MTB. Understand?"

"Yeah, I do," said Mike.

Mike lay there in his bunk—no girl tonight. He could not sleep. He didn't know what to do. Maybe if he planned it, then he'd go through with it. Sometimes people do things they normally wouldn't do when they're pushed to their limit. *Yeah, I won't worry about it. When the time comes, I'll go through with it. I'll have to. Big Al is expecting success with this mission, and you can't bribe a dead person.* Mike would have to follow through when the time came.

The day they were to hit the Los Alamos bikers came sooner rather than later. Mike was surprised and scared.

Mike, Big Al, and Charley were waiting for the Los Alamos bikers to get to the end of their partying. They had been waiting outside the gang house for over two hours. Mike's heart was beating so fast he thought it was going to jump out of his chest. Here was the moment he was dreading. He was hoping that the killer instinct would kick in when he needed it. Big Al and Charley were waiting with him, so as to witness the killing.

"Vega's people will know exactly who killed him. Let's hope that this will start Los Alamos members thinking about leaving our territory," Charley said. "If not, we'll just have to kill them all." Both men started laughing.

Mike was thinking, *What the hell am I doing here?*

At almost two in the morning, the last of the visitors had left the house. There were three Los Alamos members in the house, along with three of their girls. Jose Vega was wasted; there had been a lot of drinking and a lot of coke sniffed that night. Everyone was laughing and falling over each other. Mike, Charley, and Big Al could see them clearly.

"Okay, Mikey, it's time. They're primed and ready to die. They're so wasted. They won't even know what hit them." With that, Big Al gave Mike his gun. It felt like it weighed a hundred pounds. Mike was still waiting for his killer instinct to kick in.

"Go, Mike," said Charley.

Mike got up and started making his way toward the gang house. No one was on guard. No one was watching the perimeter of the house. It was easy pickings, really. Mike entered the house through the kitchen back door. Still no one noticed him. *Well, the desire to kill should be hitting me now,* he thought.

Nothing.

Mike raised the gun above his shoulders and pressed himself against the kitchen wall behind the door. He figured that he would kick out the door, surprise them all, shoot quickly, and leave. *Just don't look at their faces,* he kept telling himself. *Just kick, move in, pull the trigger, turn, and run out. Don't think. Just pull the trigger and run. It can't be that hard.* Mike kicked in the door, and he was right, everyone was surprised—shocked really. They just sat there. The laughing turned to silence. Mike did what he told himself not to do; he looked at their faces. In that instant, he saw a look that he had never seen before. It was a look from people who were expecting to die. No one moved.

The bad news was Mike's finger had frozen on the trigger. The good news was no one in the Los Alamos gang had a gun close to him or her.

The scene played itself out slowly. Only a few seconds had elapsed from the time Mike had kicked in the door to the scene that unfolded. All hell broke loose. Jose Vega and his crew moved toward their weapons at the same time. At that instant, the door behind Mike swung outward. Big

Al and Charley came rushing in with their guns blazing. Mike dropped his arm. When silence returned to the house, the Los Alamos members present and their girlfriends lay dead. Charley lay on the floor beside Mike's feet. He was also dead. One of the Los Alamos men had reached his gun and fired. Charley was the victim of very quick reflexes.

Mike stood in the middle of the room. He could not believe what he was looking at. He then heard the sound of a trigger being pulled beside his left ear.

"Why didn't you shoot, Mikey?" Big Al was purple with rage. "You had them all ready and waiting. What the hell is wrong with you? Charley's dead, and it's your fault. I thought you were strong enough to do this. But you let me down, Mikey. You let me down. All you had to do was pull the damn trigger. Now, you have to die. And I have to be the one to kill you. This is your fault, Mikey. Your fault."

Mike moved faster than he ever had in his life. He didn't want to die. Not here. Not now. Mike's left arm hit Big Al across the chest, surprising him. He dropped the gun. Both men lunged for the gun. They both managed to get their hands on it at the same time. Then the battle for control of the gun began. Writhing, twisting, pulling, and tugging, the two men rolled around the room. Then the sound of the shot rang loudly in the night air. Both men stopped moving. Mike Ryan was the one to stand up. Breathing heavy and labored, Mike looked down at Big Al, who was bleeding from his chest. Mike kicked the gun out of reach and stared at Big Al. Big Al managed to open his eyes for a few seconds, looked Mike straight in the eyes, and said, "You're a dead man."

Mike left the way he came in, through the back door. He sprinted across the back field and through the bushes where the three men had been waiting. A little further into the woods were their three motorcycles. Mike hopped on his motorcycle and left immediately without looking back. He heard the sound of police sirens coming from every direction.

What's wrong with me? he thought. *Why couldn't I pull that trigger? After all the shit I've seen, you'd think I could've pulled that damn trigger. Why didn't I just do what I had planned—kick and fire, kick and fire.* Even though Mike had lived the life of a bike gang member, he was not made of the same stuff that Big Al and his friends were made of.

"I'm screwed now," he said.

Chapter 6

March 2004

Big Al heard the police sirens. He was bleeding. He had to get up and get out of the house—and fast.

Mikey. I knew it. I won't make that mistake again. No one is gonna get my trust all too soon. The coward is gonna pay for this. Good ole Charley is dead because of that shithead. He's gonna pay for this.

Big Al grabbed a shirt and wrapped it around his chest to try to stop the bleeding. He didn't want to lead the cops along his escape route. He pushed through the kitchen door and made his way through the yard, the bushes, and to his bike.

He saw that Mike had already taken off on his bike.

I'll get that bastard, he thought.

He jumped on his bike, started up the engine, and took off just as the police were arriving. All they saw was his dust.

Big Al just made it to the clubhouse. He was bleeding pretty badly, but this had happened to him before, and he had survived it. He figured he would survive it again. They had a resident doctor, so he didn't have to report to a hospital and get caught by the cops. Once he healed, he would go after Mikey. And when he found him, he would take great pleasure in watching him die.

Mike Ryan had been feeling uneasy for about two years. When the feelings started, he couldn't understand them. He just knew that he was in the wrong place, doing the wrong things, and feeling the wrong feelings. He knew he had to cover his back, so he had been slicing a little money off the top each time he had gotten his hands on any money, from any source. Stealing from the gang was not tolerated and punishable by death, so he had had to be very careful with this extra money.

Mike had a bank safety deposit box and had been sneaking away to put money into it. The key was attached to the underneath of his bike. He had to act fast. His bike was well known by a lot of people. And Mike knew that Big Al would have a lot of eyes out looking for him. He had to get some clothes, get his key, get his money, and ditch the bike. In addition, he had to do it fast. He wasn't sure if Big Al had died, but he wasn't taking any chances. He knew that Big Al was a tough cookie, and he wouldn't die easily. He also knew that if Big Al lived, he would be hunting him down immediately.

Mike pulled behind a clothing store and hid his bike. He entered the store through the back door and got himself a new set of clothes, indiscreet and not flashy. He slipped out the back door again, got on his bike, and proceeded to the bank. He hid his bike again and changed in the alley beside the bank. Mike looked normal, except for the beard and long hair. He threw a hat on his head and entered the bank.

I didn't know why I was saving this money, but now I'm glad I followed my instincts, he thought. *No one else takes care of me but me. No one else cares. And no one else matters.*

There were no holdups. Mike went into the safety deposit vault and removed all of his money. He went quickly to his bike and left town forever.

He decided that it would be safer to ride at night, so Mike kept on riding until morning. He entered a fairly big town, just outside of Cincinnati, the next morning. He had to find a motorcycle shop. His plan was to talk someone into a trade. He'd trade down considerably, and then he'd be able to get rid of his beauty. He loved that bike, but everyone knew the bike. Mike had a great reputation as a bike mechanic and a rider. No one could ride a bike as well as Mike Ryan. Now he had to play down his reputation and just get rid of the bike.

The owner of the shop turned to watch the weird-looking guy ride up on the fantastic bike. It was one mother of a bike. *I wonder what he wants,* he thought.

Mike got off his bike and walked toward the interested owner. Mike could see him salivating already. Mike didn't want to look too eager. He didn't want to alert the guy to any connection with any bike gang. It might scare him, and then he wouldn't be able to unload the bike.

"Hi," Mike said.

"How you doin'?" said the owner.

"Fine, fine," said Mike. "I wonder if you can help me. A friend of mine died in an accident, and he left me this motorcycle. Well, I really like the bike, but it's way too big for me. I love riding motorcycles. I find it a lot of fun really, but I'm having trouble handling this bike."

"Yeah, how can I help you?" the owner asked.

"Well, I was wondering if anyone ever trades in a motorcycle. Hey, this motorcycle was free, so I'm not in the market to make any money. I'd just like to trade this in for a motorcycle I can ride."

Mike looked honest and stupid to the owner. *What does he mean, trade in?* he thought. The owner felt he was going to make a nice profit from this deal.

"Well, buddy, I'm in the business to sell bikes, not trade for bikes, you know."

"Yes, yes. I know," Mike said earnestly. "Maybe you can direct me to a shop that does deal with motorcycle trades?"

You asshole, Mike thought. *You know bloody well that this bike is worth a lot of money. No one has a bike like this. I could build circles around any bike in your shop. Just play it cool, Mikey. Just play it cool.*

"No, no, I didn't say we couldn't do business. I'm just not in the habit of dealing with trade-ins. What kind of bike would you be interested in?" the owner asked.

"Well, let's see now. How about this one?" asked Mike, pointing to a small but decent bike. It was worth about one-quarter of Mike's bike, at the most.

"This one? Yeah, this one is a pretty good bike. I'm not sure if this would be a straight trade-in though."

The owner looked at Mike as if he was a total idiot who knew nothing about bikes. Mike returned the look, continuing his act.

"But, you know, I'll think about it." The owner circled the bike in question.

"I'd appreciate it," Mike said. "I just want to get rid of the bike. I hurt from trying to hold up the bike, and frankly, I'm sick of it."

"I think we can make a deal here, buddy. When do you want this trade to kick in?" The owner was hoping that Mike would say right away. He needed the money this week, and this would make his bills. He knew it would take him no time to find someone to buy it—for a big profit.

"Right away," answered Mike. "I just want to get rid of it. There's nothing on it that I need. So is it a deal?"

"Yeah, yeah, okay, buddy. You've got yourself a deal."

The two men exchanged keys. Mike listened to a boring lesson on how to ride the bike. Little did the guy know that Mike could outmaneuver anyone on a bike.

Just let me outta here, he thought. *I have to get out of sight during the day.*

Mike got on his brand-new motorcycle. He thanked the owner again, started the engine, and rode slowly out of sight. Once Mike had cleared the sight of the owner, he gunned the bike. The bike lifted off the ground and took off at about half the speed of his old bike. But Mike felt good. It was a move he had felt he had to make for a few years, but he hadn't had the courage. He wasn't sure what he was gonna do now, but it had to be better than what he was running from.

Totally exhausted, he decided to pull off onto a side road and find a place to sleep. He had been up all night, and it was starting to hit him. He found a spot behind some trees. It was a beautiful day. The sun was shining, and the wind was blowing. Mike loved the wind. It always made him think he could fly. He laid the bike down, rolled his new jacket as a pillow, lay down, and fell dead asleep.

Chapter 7

The marquee read:

Elizabeth Hamilton
starring in
Giselle.

Big letters, she thought. *So big. I can't believe it. I'm actually dancing in a major production, and it's my name— my name—on the marquee. If only Gram could see this.*

Elizabeth sighed, knowing that one of the most important people in her life wouldn't be able to share the opening with her. Gram had died in her sleep six months prior to the opening of Elizabeth's first ballet in which she was the primary dancer.

Before her death, Gram was a regular visitor to rehearsals and gatherings. She was excited to watch the rehearsals. She went every day with Elizabeth; it was as if Gram could not get enough of the dance. She watched every movement and provided drinks for Elizabeth and other members of the dance troupe. She had become everyone's grandmother. She was having the time of her life. The three of them would go out to dinner at the end of a long day and talk about their days. Monique was getting so much satisfaction from her work at the magazine. They discussed the current trends in fashion and laughed at the new haute couture lines. Hideous was the opinion of all three women, which led to even more laughter. People in the restaurant would turn and stare. They looked like they were enjoying each other so much and their love was apparent. They made a striking image when they walked in anywhere—Gram with silver and white hair and long flowing skirts, Monique with her dark sleek bob, long legs, and tailored clothes, and Elizabeth with her white-blonde flowing hair and her long, sleek body, which was forever covered in white and off-white natural fibers.

The night before Elizabeth discovered her beloved Gram dead, they had gone to their favorite restaurant, Le Bistro. They had drunk a little too much wine, consuming two bottles of delicious Beaujolais. They had closed the place and taken a taxi home, arriving at 1:30 a.m. It was almost as if neither of them wanted the night to end. Elizabeth knew that she would suffer in the morning, but she had so enjoyed the evening. When she woke in the morning with a slight headache, she thought it was funny that the smell of fresh coffee wasn't filling the condo. She thought then that Gram was feeling the ill effects of too much wine as well. Her mother had already left for the office. *Nothing can slow her down,* Elizabeth thought.

Elizabeth showered and gave Gram a few more minutes of sleep before it was time to leave. When she knocked on Gram's door, she felt guilty. She thought maybe she should let her sleep in and come to the rehearsal a little later. However, she knew better. Gram wanted to be with her on the way to the studio and from the studio. She knew Gram would not like it if Elizabeth left without her. So she knocked, and she knocked again. There was no answer. *That's strange,* she thought. Elizabeth slowly entered Gram's room to find Gram sleeping soundly on the bed. She looked so peaceful, Elizabeth was thinking as she reached forward to give Gram's shoulder a little shake. As soon as she touched her, Elizabeth knew she had lost her most precious grandmother. Gram's shoulder was cold and did not move with the nudge. Her face and body position portrayed a relaxed and happy woman. Her white hair lay softly on the pillow, and the duvet was gathered around her neck, held in place with her beautiful hands.

Elizabeth felt her heart stop. She had to sit on the chair beside the bed to catch her breath. "Oh, Gram," she said, "why did you leave me? I still need you." But it was not to be. Elizabeth had to make the hardest phone call of her life. She had to phone Monique and tell her that her best friend and mother had died in her sleep. Monique had rushed immediately home, and life for the Hamilton women was never the same again.

Elizabeth was dreading the reading of Gram's will. *Who cares who got what? I just want Gram back,* Elizabeth thought. Monique had explained that it would be an insult to her mother not to attend the reading of her last wishes. Elizabeth reluctantly joined her mother in the lawyer's office.

There were the usual financial bequeaths explained by the lawyer. Gram had invested some money and accumulated a little wealth. She had added to her last request the reading of a letter to "her girls."

Elizabeth was glad that she accompanied her mother. It would difficult to sit alone and hear the last request of someone so dear to you. But the words were comforting. Gram described how much Monique and Elizabeth completed her life. They looked at each other and laughed through their tears. Gram stated that she would always be with them in spirit. Elizabeth could practically feel her in the room.

The last part of Gram's will dealt with the cottage.

Gram had bequeathed the deed of the cottage property to Elizabeth. She added that she wanted Elizabeth to have a place to return to for security and solace.

Elizabeth and her mother left the lawyer's office solemnly. They ached with grief. Both women then threw themselves into their work to occupy their minds and assuage their grief.

Monique and Elizabeth did not go to the cottage after Gram's death. They couldn't bring themselves to be there, without Gram with them. It had been their special place where they went together on short holidays. They now spent the holidays in the city, like most of the city folk. No more water, no more dock, and no more Gram.

Everyone had forgotten about the cottage. No one had visited the property for five years, until Elizabeth decided that if she did not go to the place of security and solace, as Gram had suggested, she surely would die herself.

Chapter 8

Late July 2004

Elizabeth woke up refreshed to the "sounds of the cottage," as she called it. She could hear the water lapping on the shore and the dock. The birds were chirping and probably circling the birdbath that Gram had put outside the mudroom, and the wind was blowing softly through the window, making her lace curtains flap up and down against the wall. These were the sounds that made her feel safe and at home.

Then reality hit her. There was a man downstairs—a very stubborn man—who was determined to reinjure himself. She did not understand why he did not want her to sleep beside him. She had slept on a few floors, and it never bothered her.

Oh well, she thought. *If he's determined to die, what am I supposed to do about it?*

She changed into her bathing suit, grabbed her beach towel, and headed downstairs. She was going to take a dip in the lake and swim out to the island and back to wake herself up.

The water will feel good. Those were her last thoughts as she went down the stairs.

Mike had been awake for about half an hour, and he had been trying to figure out how he was going to get himself upright in bed and get his feet on the ground. Then he heard her footsteps upstairs. He turned his head to see her glide down the stairs. Her long legs were stretching for the steps, and they looked lean and athletic in that black bathing suit. It accentuated her blonde hair and showed just enough of her body to make a man want to see more. He kept quiet, and she went straight down and out the door, without looking in his direction. He was glad because she would've seen a look of awe on his face, and he certainly didn't want her to know what kind of effect she was starting to have on his psyche.

"Enough of this shit," he said.

Concentrate on getting up, he thought. *Enough.*

He heard her body hit the water and wondered what she looked like moving through the water. *Concentrate.* It took Mike fifteen pain-filled minutes to sit up. Every muscle in his abdomen and back resisted the move. The muscles had not moved for weeks, and there were still bruises from the severe beating he had endured. He could still hear Big Al laughing and felt the fists hitting him again. He'd have to put that behind him now.

Mike sat up and could see out the window onto the lake. He squinted but could not see any sign of Elizabeth. He knew she was out there because he had heard her dive in, but he would have to stand to see further into the lake. "Well, that'll give me another reason to stand up," he said. He grabbed onto the side table and used all the strength in his body, but he could not muster up the strength and energy to get up off the bed. He didn't give up, though. He was stubborn, as Elizabeth had thought earlier. He grunted and moaned while trying with all his might to get his body off the bed.

He had not even noticed that Elizabeth had returned from her swim, entered the front door, and stood staring at him.

"If you moan any louder, you're going to scare all the animals far, far away from this place."

She scared the crap out of Mike. He just about jumped out of his drawers.

"What the hell are you doing sneaking up on me like that?"

"I was simply returning from my swim. When I rose out of the water, I could hear you from the dock, moaning. I thought someone was hurting you again."

"I'm sorry, but it hurts. Okay, I'll admit it. I can't get myself up, and it hurts like hell to try. But I am getting up today or I'll die trying."

"Would you like me to help?" Elizabeth asked.

"No."

Mike tried again and again. He had no success and was completely exhausted.

Elizabeth had gone upstairs to change out of her bathing suit. She could hear him moaning and screaming downstairs and shook her head in despair.

I guess I'll have to let him keep trying. I have to have patience, she told herself. She put on a pretty, pink cotton summer dress. She thought she looked pretty good. She slipped on flip-flops and went downstairs to see a very exhausted, sweaty man sitting on the side of the bed with his hands holding his ribs. Michael Ryan was breathing heavy and labored. Her heart melted. He looked like a little boy who had gotten hurt while playing outside with his buddies and still did not want to come into the house.

Elizabeth walked past him and the bed and went to the kitchen. Running some water, she put the kettle on for breakfast, got the eggs and bacon from the fridge, and got some pumpernickel for toast. She turned to look at Mike and said, "Would you like to try eating some soft, fried eggs, and I could cut up small pieces of toast?"

Mike looked at her. He was in such pain. He cleared his throat, licked his parched lips, and said, "Yeah, that would be okay."

"I can run you some nice warm water to bathe with, if you'd like. Would you like some help getting up and maybe getting to the bathroom?"

The bathroom, he thought. He had found it a little degrading and humiliating to have Elizabeth use a bed pan and see him going to the bathroom the last couple of days.

No one, he had thought. *No one had ever seen me in that situation, ever.* Being able to go to the bathroom himself and not have some woman help him was enough incentive for him to reply, "Yes, help me there, and I can do the rest."

Elizabeth put down the dishcloth and went over to the bed. She may have been very thin, but she was still strong. All those hours of training did not go to waste. She had built a well-oiled machine that was still capable of work. Mike grunted, and Elizabeth pulled and pushed. He made it to his feet. *There,* he thought. *I finally got out of that freaking bed.*

"Well, we're one big step further to getting you to the bathroom now. However, we have to go slowly, so as not to injure you. You're still healing, and I'm sure this is hurting."

No comment from Mike.

Very slowly, they made their way around the bed and to the back of the cottage where the bathroom was located. Mike told Elizabeth that he was glad to have finally gotten out of the bed and that it felt good that he could do something for himself. When his hand felt the doorknob, it was as if he had won the lottery. He was so happy.

Elizabeth helped Mike into the bathroom. There were towels and toiletries already available to him, so all she had to do was close the door.

"Call me when you're ready, and I'll help you back to bed. Please don't try to move around yourself. I'm even worried about leaving you alone in here."

"I'm fine," Mike said. "I'll call you when I'm finished."

It took over half an hour for Mike to do his business and clean up a little. He ran the water in the sink, while sitting on the toilet, and managed to get a face cloth to wipe himself off. The clean water felt great, and soap smelled so good to him. He was so glad that he was doing his morning ritual by himself. He even brushed his teeth. He made note of the fact that she had left a new toothbrush there, still in the package, with toothpaste for his use. He didn't understand her generosity. He had never encountered a generous soul in his life. At least, he couldn't remember having done so. She had shaved off his beard. His hair was still scruffy and dirty, but his face was clean-shaven. He looked so different. Mike hadn't seen his cheeks and chin for years. *Enough of that,* he thought. It was time to get moving. He was so tired, however.

He sat on the toilet in blue boxer shorts, waiting to be helped back to bed. "I'm finished," he called out.

"Okay," Elizabeth answered from the kitchen. She had been sitting there for twenty minutes, waiting to hear him ask for help. The eggs were done and on the stove, and the bread was ready to be popped into the toaster. The smell of bacon filled the cottage, and the smell of the fresh coffee topped it off.

Elizabeth stopped outside the door and asked, "Is it okay if I open the door?"

"Yeah, yeah," answered Mike.

Elizabeth turned the knob and entered the bathroom. She saw a very tired but cleaner man staring at her. She still marveled at the blueness of his eyes. She wished she could wave a wand and get rid of his hair, but she looked past all of that into a pair of tired—and beautiful—blue eyes.

They slowly made their way back to the bed. Mike let out a few moans on the way. He couldn't help it. Elizabeth apologized. Mike told her not to worry. He continued to moan, and she continued to apologize all the way across the room. She helped him into bed and propped him up on four pillows so that she could place a tray in front of him.

Those pillows and that bed had never felt so good. He could not believe how sore he was and how good he felt to be back in that stupid bed. He gave up and sat there waiting to be served some food. He realized that he was indeed hungry. All that work, just to go to the bloody bathroom, had built up his appetite. He didn't like the realization that he needed this woman. He depended on her right now to make sure that he continued to eat, continued to be safe, and continued to be clean. He had depended on one other person in his life—his mother. Since her death, there had been only one person Michael Ryan trusted—and that was Michael Ryan.

Elizabeth got Michael some orange juice and some painkillers. She came over to the bed before bringing him his food and handed him the juice and the pills.

Thank God, he thought. *I've never wanted pills so much in my life. I am not going to complain.* "Thanks," he said.

"You're welcome," replied Elizabeth, and she turned to get breakfast served. She put down a plate with some bacon, all cut up, and some eggs, all cut up. There was soft toast sliced in long strips, making it quite easy for Mike to feed himself.

How did she know? he said to himself.

"I'll just get my food and sit in Gram's rocking chair and join you," she said.

Gram's chair. This must be her family's cottage, he thought. *Hmm, interesting.*

They sat and they ate in silence. It took Mike awhile to eat the breakfast. He did fairly well. He managed to eat about three-quarters of what Elizabeth had prepared. The juice felt like nectar going down. He could feel a little bit of life running through his veins. Nevertheless, at the end of the meal, he was exhausted. He could barely talk.

"Thanks," he said to Elizabeth as she cleared his tray.

"No problem," she replied. She placed his tray on the side table, removed two of the pillows, and helped Mike lay down in the bed. Moving away softly, Elizabeth smiled as he fell asleep.

He's exhausted, she thought. *He tried too much and too soon.*

Putting herself in his place, she knew that she would have tried to move and get out of bed as soon as possible. She knew one could move through pain. She understood Mr. Michael Ryan and his yearning for fending for himself. She had a little stubborn streak in herself as well.

She turned to clean up after breakfast. It took awhile to clean up. With the wonderful fruit she had bought at the market, she prepared some fruit salad and placed it in the fridge. It had been difficult to come up with meals that Mike would have no trouble eating. She decided to make him a smoothie with lots of fruit and yogurt for lunch, if he woke up for lunch. It would be refreshing and easy to swallow.

It was a beautiful July day, so she grabbed her current book and went on the deck to look at the lake and get some reading done. This was Elizabeth's healing time. This was the place in the world where she felt at peace within herself. Her body returned to the past when she sat on that dock—no stress, just relaxation. Gram had created this perfect little corner of the world for them. It was giving her exactly what she needed at this point. Her grandmother had bequeathed a most precious gift to Elizabeth. Elizabeth knew that she had made the right decision in returning to the cottage. She could feel Gram smiling down upon her and approving. She thought that Gram would even approve of the presence of Michael Ryan. She, herself, had been kind to others throughout her life. Elizabeth had felt Gram's spirit guide her through the last few weeks. She enjoyed her afternoon.

Chapter 9

July 2004

Mike didn't wake up for lunch. He slept through midmorning and the afternoon. He started to stir at about six o'clock.

Elizabeth had gone into town for some supplies. She had left a note. When she returned, Mike was still sleeping. She removed the note and quietly put her purchases away. She busied herself by cleaning up a little, sat in the rocking chair at one point, and just stared at Michael Ryan. She was thinking about the beating and wondered why they had beaten him up. She also wondered why a grown man would be part of a biker gang. Looking into those blue eyes was not an uneasy thing. However, she saw pain—not physical pain. She saw emotional pain and tried to figure out what it was that she was seeing exactly. She admonished herself for even thinking about such things. It was none of her business. Moreover, who did she think she was—a psychologist? She had enough to deal with in her own life.

Just before Gram's death, Elizabeth had felt that her life was perfect. She had a loving mother and grandmother. Her career had been peaking; she was in the midst of rehearsals for her first prima ballerina role in the ballet,

Giselle. Her partner in life was her partner on the stage. They had identical lifestyles, identical goals, and they had developed a special bond—on the stage and in real life. Peter had fit right into her small family. Both her mother and grandmother had embraced him immediately.

However, her life was now upside down.

She had thrown it all away. She had felt that something was missing. She did not know what was missing, but as the days went by, she felt more and more detached from the world in which she had been living. She no longer felt happiness. She no longer had the normal inner drive for perfection; she had been feeling as if she was going to explode. Her body and especially her mind needed a rest— needed peace.

She had come to the cottage in search of peace. She realized this as she sat and rocked in Gram's chair watching Michael Ryan sleep.

Chapter 10

May 2003

There was a standing ovation at the end of the ballet. The members of the dance troupe came out one by one to be acknowledged, and the crowd kept on clapping. Peter Rogers came out second to last to thunderous applause.

Peter, with his blond hair and blue eyes, was the perfect ballet partner for Elizabeth. Their bodies jelled together on the stage. Peter could jump and turn in the air with bursts of strength and in the next instant, gently lift Elizabeth and turn her in a perfect pose. They both looked ethereal, yet they demonstrated great strength and beauty.

Elizabeth came out of the wings delicately. She had tears in her eyes. She could hear the applause, and she could see Peter, but her mind was on her mother and missing Gram. She saw her mother in the front row. Monique was wiping away tears and had a big smile on her face. She, too, was thinking that Elizabeth deserved every second of this stardom. Elizabeth took Peter's hand and slowly bowed. He bowed and accepted the accolades with a huge smile. He was exhausted but could not believe the thrill he was having at this moment. A junior dancer came out and presented her with the biggest bouquet of roses she had ever seen. She bowed again, turned to acknowledge the rest of the dance troupe, bowed, and left the stage on Peter's arm.

Peter Rogers had become very important in Elizabeth's life. On the day of Gram's death, he had come over to the condo as soon as he heard that she had passed away. Elizabeth had phoned the rehearsal hall to say that she would not be coming to dance. Everyone was granted a few days of vacation as Elizabeth and Monique dealt with Gram's death. The director had agreed with her, and all the dancers went home to relax for a few days. Peter left the rehearsal studio and went straight to Elizabeth's home. He had been invited to dinner on many occasions and knew how much she would be hurting, and he wanted to be there. She had become more than a partner to him. To be Elizabeth Hamilton's partner was a great honor for him. He knew that being paired with her would catapult his career. Now he had developed feelings for her beyond the stage. His fingers tingled after he touched her while they danced. To meet a woman with the same passion for ballet was a dream come true for Peter. She was a beautiful, honest, and hardworking woman. He loved the touch of her body and the flexing of her muscles when they danced. He had been trying to get the courage to suggest to Elizabeth that their relationship should begin a secondary path—they should now become a couple and not just a duo. He had not had the courage yet. Now he had to help her through this most trying time.

Peter knocked on the door three times before Monique opened it. She had tissue in her hands, and it was easy to tell that she had been crying. She waved him in. He reached over and gave her a hug, which Monique returned, but then she turned quickly and hurried away. Peter stood in the doorway and wasn't sure what to do. He closed the door and walked slowly down the hallway. He didn't want to call out her name because he wasn't sure where she was, and this wasn't a time to go around yelling. He found her rocking in a chair beside her grandmother's bed. He froze. He had not really seen a dead person, other than in a coffin. Seeing Gram in the bed unnerved him, but he had to keep it together. He walked slowly into the room, knelt down on one knee beside the rocking chair, and put one hand on Elizabeth's hand. He didn't say anything. He just gave her hand a squeeze. She squeezed back and kept looking at Gram.

She finally broke the silence. "They haven't come to get her yet. Supposedly the funeral home people and a doctor come together. The doctor has to declare the cause of death before anyone can move her. If it's determined that it's natural causes, then the funeral director will take over and follow Mom's instructions. Mom said Gram had all her wishes written down in a letter, so she was just to give it to the specified funeral director." Peter listened in silence. "Gram made all arrangements years ago. She said that she didn't want people worrying about arrangements. She just wanted everyone to celebrate her life."

Elizabeth turned and looked at Peter, and giant tears ran down her cheeks. With every blink, more tears flowed. Elizabeth was fighting to hold herself together.

"I didn't want to leave her alone," she added. "Mom is just pacing around the apartment."

"I'm sorry," Peter said. "I know how much your grandmother meant to you. Just tell me what I can do for you, and I'll do it. I hope I'm not intruding, but I felt I had to be here with you."

"I don't feel you're intruding at all," Elizabeth replied. "I'm so glad you came. I didn't know that I needed someone to lean on, until your hand touched me. My mother will need me right now. Thank you for coming. You're just what I need."

Peter exhaled. He hadn't been sure about coming and had doubted his decision all the way up the elevator, but now he was certain that he was in the right place.

The doorbell rang, and they heard Monique rush to the door. It was the doctor, the funeral director and his staff, and a police officer. Their arrival just about made Monique faint. Elizabeth could see her mother's heart tearing apart. She knew how they had depended on each other over the years. Elizabeth knew her mother was now going into a mode where she could function properly and get the arrangements made for *her* mother. Elizabeth didn't want to feel, either; just to get through the next few days was the plan.

Without saying a word, Monique led the way to Gram's bedroom. When she came through the door, Peter stood up. Elizabeth stayed seated and did not look up.

She thought, *If I don't look up and see those people, then maybe this really didn't happen.*

"Honey," Monique said, "the doctor has to examine Gram so that Gram's wishes can be carried out. Maybe we should just step out of the room and wait in the family room?"

Elizabeth was shaking. She wasn't sure her legs would hold her when she got up. Peter sensed her apprehension, so he reached under her arms and helped her up. She was shaky but managed to stand. She leaned over, brushed some hair off of her grandmother's forehead, and kissed her gently before turning and leaving the room. With Peter's help, she made it out of the room, through the family room, and onto the balcony. She felt like she could not breathe. Her mother followed them.

The two women faced each other, grabbed each other, and burst into tears. Peter ran to get them both some water and more tissue. He placed both on the table, sat in a chair, and respected their need for each other.

The police officer cleared his throat. Peter, Monique, and Elizabeth turned to look at him.

"The doctor has finished his examination. It seems your mother passed away from natural causes. We see no need for an autopsy at this time. Mr. Brown, the funeral director, is waiting for your instructions."

"Yes, thank you," said Monique while she tried to stop crying. "I'll be right there."

Both women took a deep breath. "Oh, God," said Elizabeth. "This is so hard. Mom, are you okay to go speak to this man?"

"Yes, dear. Gram had everything arranged. She left complete instructions. She and I talked it all over. I tried to tell her that I didn't want to discuss such gruesome things, but she insisted. She said it would be easier on you and me if we understood her wishes and just followed the plan. The plan was to go to her desk and get out a letter she had written to me with the name of the funeral home. I'm to give them a letter with her instructions, a copy of which they already have in their files, and I'm to let them take care of everything. My job, she said, was to respect her wishes and take care of you."

With that, Monique left the balcony. She went directly to Gram's room. She took the instructions off the top of the desk and handed them to Mr. Brown.

Mr. Brown already knew what to do. When Monique had called him, he had gone into his files and read over Constance Hamilton's wishes. All the arrangements had been discussed and paid for.

Monique turned to look at her beautiful mother. She leaned over and gave her mother her last hug. She could barely let go. She wasn't sure how long she had been holding Constance Elizabeth Hamilton, but she felt Elizabeth touch her arm and say, "Mom, it's time." Monique kissed her mother on the cheek, left the room, went directly to her room, and shut the door quietly.

Elizabeth kissed Gram again. She got up and looked at Peter. Her eyes said, "Please take over." Peter escorted Elizabeth to the family room and returned to the bedroom.

"Thank you for your patience, everyone," Peter began. "Ms. Hamilton has given you the wishes of her mother, and I'm sure you'll carry them out. Would you please call her tomorrow?"

"Yes, of course," Mr. Brown said.

"If you would please hurry with whatever it is you have to do. I'm sure both women are just dreading the time until you leave with her body."

"Yes, I'm sure. We'll be as discreet and quick as possible. Please tell Ms. Hamilton that we'll contact her as soon as possible."

It took about thirty minutes for them to prepare and remove Gram's body. The sound of the gurney was eerie as it rolled down the hallway. Elizabeth shuddered at the sound. She didn't think she could live through this, but she knew she had to be strong for Monique. This would affect her mother greatly, she thought.

Both women heard the front door shut, and both women gave a heavy sigh. The retreat of the strangers gave them the green light to release their pain. Peter sat and held Elizabeth as she sobbed. He rubbed her hair and her face. Wiping tears from her cheeks was very comforting to Elizabeth. Monique was sobbing in her bedroom.

Life, for all of them, would now be very different.

"I'm here for as long as you need me," Peter whispered.

Elizabeth just hugged him tighter. His understanding and concern were so appreciated and so needed. She needed to be held right now. Peter's love for her was very evident now. Realizing this was soothing; she needed to fill the void in her heart.

Without her saying a word, Peter was happy that he could finally reveal the love he felt for Elizabeth. He was sorry that it had taken such a tragic event to be able to show how he felt.

"I can't thank you enough for your help today."

"I'm here for as long as you need me and for whatever you need me to do. Just try to relax and rest."

"I should see about my mother."

"I think she needs this time alone. She cried for quite a while, so I think she may have fallen asleep. Maybe it would be better to let her rest. What do you think?"

"You're probably right. Maybe I'll just snuggle in a little more, if you don't mind."

"Snuggle away."

Elizabeth sobbed quietly for about twenty more minutes and then dozed off. Peter was holding onto her with all the love he had in his heart. He knew losing Gram was a very important moment in Elizabeth's life.

Chapter 11

February 2004

It was February, and Monique had announced to Elizabeth that she would be heading off to Paris and Rome for a two-week work/vacation. She mentioned to Elizabeth that she was worried about leaving her alone. Elizabeth assured her that she would be fine. She had her work, and she had Peter. Monique was satisfied and made her arrangements; she would be traveling to Europe alone.

"So, if you get an offer on the condo, you can text me right away. I have given you the power of attorney for the sale. I hate to let go of the condo, but we don't need all that room now," said Monique.

"This is prime real estate, Mom. I'm sure it won't be long before we sell the condo. I have to start looking for my own first real apartment."

"If we have to bunk in with each other until we get our own places, at least we know we can live together."

Both women laughed. They had been living together in harmony for years. The major factor in selling the condo was that it reminded both of them that Gram's room was empty.

It was time to move on. They could afford to upgrade their living quarters now. Constance had left them a little nest egg, and they were both doing well in their careers. It was going to be an exciting summer. The new ballet was opening July Fourth weekend. They would have the end of May and all of June to find a new place.

It was the fashion season in Paris, and Monique needed to see the up and coming new fashions for the coming year. Many times, her mother and/or Elizabeth had accompanied her to Paris, and they had a great trip. Monique had come to trust Peter; he would take care of Elizabeth. Time heals all wounds, but time was healing slowly.

Elizabeth made plans for the night of Monique's departure. She figured that it was time for her to forge ahead with her life. Her grandmother would have wanted her to do that. She did not believe in focusing on the past.

Chapter 12

Peter
April 2004

Peter could not believe that such a beautiful woman, at the age of twenty-four, was still a virgin. He and Elizabeth had gotten very close since her grandmother's death. Losing Gram had affected her intensely. She was suffering, and there wasn't anything he could do but be there when she needed someone to lean on.

He had fallen hard. He didn't expect it, as she was "just his partner," but it had happened. She moved like an angel across the stage. When she danced, he stood and watched, mesmerized. He was having erotic dreams about her and knew he had to go slowly because she had never given herself to another man. He did not want to spoil her moment, but he was getting antsy. He wanted to commit body and soul into this relationship.

"I do really hate to leave you every night," said Peter as he looked into Elizabeth's beautiful green eyes.

"I know," she replied. "But we'll have some alone time soon. My mother is leaving for Paris, and it will all work out."

Elizabeth had decided that now would be the time for her to embark on her individual phase, fully becoming a woman.

On the eve after Monique's departure for Paris, Elizabeth invited Peter over for dinner. She had planned a great meal and was having it catered, because they would be dancing until six and she would not have time to whip up a dinner—especially a special dinner. They didn't change after rehearsal; they went directly to the apartment, as they were both famished.

Peter was totally surprised. The caterer had set a special dinner table, with candelabra. There had been extra candles lit throughout the dining room. Their dining room table was a small, round table that sat only two people, so it was easy for the caterer to make it look like a cozy, intimate dinner for two. They had set the table and left dinner warming in the kitchen. No one was in the apartment when they arrived, so upon entering the dining room, Peter was shocked.

"I thought we would have a special dinner tonight," Elizabeth explained.

"I can see that," he said.

"So if you'll just have a seat, I'll get dinner, and you can open the champagne." The caterer had left a beautiful bottle of champagne chilling beside the table.

"I can do that," said Peter.

Elizabeth left for the kitchen. The dinner was all prepared, as she had asked. The dessert of chocolate soufflé was sitting in the fridge. She removed the covers and took the two plates to the table. Peter had already uncorked the champagne and was waiting for Elizabeth so that he could pour the drinks.

For the first time in her life, Elizabeth was considering making love to a man. She had never experienced such feelings. She worked too hard during her teens and really didn't have enough time for an emotional and/or sexual relationship. It never really crossed her mind, but it was crossing her mind now. She knew that Peter had been exceptionally patient. A feeling of anticipation emanated from Peter when they were together now, and they were together all the time, except at bedtime. He would kiss her sweetly and head home if they were at the apartment. Or they would kiss goodnight at a restaurant and head their separate ways, until the morning.

"And what shall we toast, my sneaky girl?"

"Oh, I was thinking that we could toast the next step in our relationship."

"Live your life the fullest," Gram always said, Elizabeth was thinking. Was she living her life to the fullest? Was there more than just dancing, eating, and sleeping? She had been having these thoughts off and on for weeks. She figured it was because she was heading into another phase, and that phase was starting to include Peter.

He had been a blessing. He was patient and kind. She was starting to have feelings beyond friendship for him. When he lifted her on the dance floor, she felt every spot where his fingers were touching her body.

Peter swallowed hard and looked directly into her beautiful green eyes. He knew what she meant and could see it in her eyes. She had finally decided to make a commitment and take that step. His heart just about leapt out of his chest. Could he contain himself through a meal?

"Well, my beauty, if that's what you'd like to toast, then that's exactly what we'll do. Let us toast to our future together."

"Yes," said Elizabeth. "Let's toast to our hearts and our bodies."

Neither of them tasted any of the wonderful food that was prepared for them. They didn't speak much. They were both hungry, and yet the food didn't seem to satisfy their appetite. They each consumed two glasses of champagne with their dinner, and after such a hard day, it did not take long for the alcohol to take effect.

When they were finished eating, Elizabeth got up to clear the table and headed off to the kitchen to get dessert. She put the plates on the counter and caught her breath as Peter turned her quickly around to face him.

"I don't think I can wait any longer," he declared. "I'm not really in the mood for dessert."

As he said that, he swept Elizabeth off her feet and headed straight to her bedroom. He lowered her gently to the floor, as usual, and stood staring at her. She was a little intimidated by his bold move, but she loved it. Both their hearts were beating wildly.

"Shall we take a shower?" Peter asked.

"Together?"

"Of course, together. And it would give me great pleasure to start off the next step in our relationship."

Elizabeth took a step back, looked Peter Rogers in the eyes, and said, "Yes, I would like that." She couldn't believe she had said that, but she was so glad that she did.

He undressed her slowly and drank in every inch of her body. She was even more beautiful than he had imagined. Her body was pale and delicate, but you could see the strength and the tightness of the muscles. He quickly took off his clothes so that Elizabeth wouldn't feel embarrassed to be the only one nude. She looked scared, he thought.

Elizabeth had seen Peter undressed before. They often changed during a performance, and clothes went on and off quite quickly. But this was different. She tingled as she looked at him. His muscles were taut and had just the right amount of bulk. She particularly liked his tush. Now, she felt a whole different sensation. She knew that she had waited for just this moment.

He took her hand and kissed it and led her to the shower. He made sure that the temperature was just right and then escorted her in. It started off awkward at first. They weren't sure what to do with the soap. Would they wash their own hair or have their partner wash it for them? Who stood where?

But nature took its course. Peter was looking at the most beautiful body in the world to him. Touching her and lifting her in the air was nothing compared to feeling and touching her smooth skin.

Elizabeth thought she would feel self-conscious being naked in front of Peter. It was the opposite. The look in his eyes put her at ease. There are not many things a male ballet dancer can hide in his leotard, but it was much more evocative to look at his muscular and strong body in the nude. To Elizabeth, he was the perfect specimen of a man, and she couldn't believe what his touch was doing to her body and her mind.

They were soon in sync with each other, just as they were on the dance floor. They rubbed soap on each other, and excitement started to rise as they touched pleasure points. She washed the small of his back and let her hands fall down onto his backside. Peter inhaled when her hands went there. Beginning with her hair, Peter moved down to her back and turned her around to wash her breasts. Elizabeth's eyes closed, and she shuddered. With the washing finished, the kissing began and lingered. Peter couldn't get enough of her. Elizabeth had never been touched like this; she was amazed and scared. She hoped that she would not disappoint Peter.

Peter, on the other hand, had no intentions of rushing. He had waited, and he could still wait. He wanted Elizabeth to desire him as much as he had desired her. He wanted to make sure she was ready for this next step in their relationship.

He dried her off and then dried himself off. Both man and woman looked magnificent. Her long, slender body was glistening, and his body was starting to show signs of being aroused. Elizabeth's heart rate had risen continuously from the start of the shower. Peter led her to her bed. Elizabeth had bought new sheets and bedding for this special night. The bed looked like a big, fluffy, white cushion. Peter drew back the duvet and the crisp cotton sheets, and Elizabeth got into the bed. Peter moved in beside her.

Slowly his hand touched her body—touched her in all the right spots. He was waiting for her to give him a sign that she was ready. He kissed her mouth, her face, her neck, and moved down to her breasts. Elizabeth could not believe what she was feeling. Everything tingled. Every inch of her body seemed ready to jump out of her skin. He was making her feel so good that she could not contain herself. She let out a slow moan.

Now Peter knew that she was getting ready for him. He wanted her to be eager; he wanted her to ask for him.

His mouth moved down her body, and he slowly spread her legs and slowly came upon her most private and most desirous spot. At that moment, Elizabeth arched her back and moaned again. *Slowly,* he thought. *Don't rush it.*

Peter brought Elizabeth to heights she had not imagined. She had heard about such feelings but had not thought she could feel this good. Then the moment came that Peter had been waiting for.

"Please, Peter," she said. "Please."

Peter drew himself up and as gently as possible entered Elizabeth's body. Fireworks went off in both of their hearts and brains. After a few strokes, they started to move in unison. Peter wanted Elizabeth to reach her peak, and then he would allow himself to peak as well. It did not take long. Elizabeth had been primed, and she was now willing, very willing. They reached their peak together. Elizabeth let out a cry, and Peter said, "Oh God."

They were stuck together. Perspiration covered both of their bodies. They were both breathing as hard as they did after a long dance. Peter lay gently on Elizabeth and then propped himself up on his hands and lay beside her.

"I hope I didn't hurt you," he said.

"No, no you didn't hurt me."

With that statement, Elizabeth started to cry. The moment had been so real and so meaningful to her that she let out all her emotions. Peter put his arm around her. He wasn't sure if he had hurt her or not. He just held onto her until she stopped crying.

"Please don't be upset," he implored.

"I'm fine," she said. "Those were tears of joy, Peter. You didn't hurt me. I'm not that fragile, you know. I just could not believe anything could be so great."

"Thank God. I was holding onto you and wondering how I could fix things."

"Well," she said, "I know exactly how you could fix things."

And with that, the fixing began . . . and did so once again that evening. By four in the morning, the two lovers were exhausted and fell soundly asleep—with smiles on their faces. Another chapter in Elizabeth's life had begun.

Chapter 13

July 2004

Mike slowly opened his eyes. As he focused, he could see Elizabeth sitting in the rocking chair looking at him.

"Welcome back," she said.

"Yeah, sure."

He tried to get up, but sitting up was not easy. Elizabeth got up and supported his back as he sat up. She put a few extra pillows behind him.

"There, that's better."

"Thanks."

"I've something for dinner all ready. I'm afraid you slept through lunch and the afternoon."

"What?"

"Yes, I guess your body needed the rest. I've made some cream of mushroom soup, and you can have a nice fruit smoothie for dessert."

That made Mike realize how hungry he indeed was. But he had to get up and go to the washroom, and he knew he would have to depend on her for help again. That bothered him. He wanted to be able to move on his own, but he could not.

"I'd like to wash up before dinner," he said.

"Yes, yes, of course. Here, I'll help you up, and we'll get you to the washroom."

Elizabeth knew that Mr. Ryan did not like depending on her and needing her support. He would have to swallow his pride for a while, because he had been badly hurt and still was not healed. It had been over nine weeks, and his body was still suffering, as well as his mind. She could see the look of frustration on his face.

"I'm not sure that I like this part of healing right now," Mike muttered.

"Well, I can understand that," replied Elizabeth. "I don't like people doting on me and watching every move when I get injured. But as my Gram once told me, sometimes in your life, you have to accept help or give help. Well, right now, I guess I'm the giver, and you will have to be the acceptor. We have to work together here to get you back on your feet. It's the way my grandmother would have treated you, especially here at the cottage."

Gram always treated strangers with kindness and care, thought Elizabeth.

Mike didn't bother to answer. Answering would have involved effort, and right now it was enough effort to get across the bloody room.

They hobbled their way across the room, to the back of the house and the washroom. Mike was happy again when the door closed. He felt so vulnerable outside of the washroom.

Elizabeth turned the heat up on the soup and broke apart saltines so that it would be easier for Mike to add them to his dinner, if he wanted. She made separate trays again, and everything was ready when Mike called to say that he was ready to go back to bed.

They had an exceptionally quiet meal. Both seemed to be lost in their thoughts. Neither one realized that they were thinking of the other.

Mike noticed the little extras that Elizabeth did to make life easier for him. She had chosen the soup, he thought, because she knew that it would be easy for him to eat. She even broke up the crackers for him. *Who does things like this?* She had put a little flower on the tray, and everything looked so pretty . . . just like her. He could feel her presence in the rocking chair beside him. He pushed back his thoughts. She was having an effect on him that he didn't like.

Elizabeth ate her meal quietly. She hoped that she had made a meal Mike could handle and one that would give him the nutrients he needed. She stopped herself from helping him. She knew that he wanted to try to do things on his own, so she let him struggle. A few times, she smiled because she heard him swear to himself under his breath. He was trying hard not to lose his temper, she thought. *I wonder what kind of man Michael Ryan truly is.*

Elizabeth cleared her tray and then got Mike's tray from him. She opened up the curtains in the big window so that Mike could see out. It was nearing eight o'clock, and the sun was starting its descent. The lake was shining, and the night sounds were beginning. Crickets were chirping loudly, and the water was lapping on the shore of the dock. Birds were flying slowly around the lake, and pretty soon they would hear the sound of the loons. She busied herself cleaning up the kitchen.

Mike sat there feeling pretty good. The meal had hit the right spot and seemed to give him some energy. He leaned against the pillows, which reduced the pain in his ribs, and looked out the window. He couldn't help, however, stealing glances toward the kitchen. She moved so effortlessly and with such grace. She was meticulous as to where things were returned and how she left the kitchen. He noticed that her last move was always folding the dish-drying cloth and laying it across the faucet to dry. He had to keep looking out the window. He didn't want her to know that he had been looking at her.

I'm comfortable, he was thinking. *I'm actually comfortable, and I feel at ease about it all. I don't have to pretend to be anyone I'm not, and I don't have to party and party and party.* He had become quite tired of the gang life. He saw no purpose to the goings on, and he had been feeling dissatisfied with life and himself. That's what started all this trouble.

Chapter 14

June 2004

Big Al healed quite well. The resident doctor had done a fine job removing the bullet and dressing his wound. The entire gang had to relocate. They had bought a house just outside of Cincinnati. This time they chose a spot that was a little more secluded. Big Al had insisted on their practicing more security procedures. He wanted lookouts at all times, just in case.

He was still wondering, however, what had happened to Mike. No one had seen his bike around. No one had reported seeing Mike. He knew that someone could not just disappear off the face of the earth. *He's pretty smart,* he thought, *and stupid. If he thinks that I'm just gonna forget about it and let him get away with his betrayal—he's barking up the wrong tree.*

Curiosity got the better of him after he had healed, and he headed off to try to find the spot where he last saw the coward. Big Al and a couple of bikers headed off into the country. They now lived closer to where they had beaten up Mike, so that was a good thing.

They drove up and down a stretch of the road for a while, not finding any trace of Mike or the scene of the fight. They concentrated their efforts on the areas just off the sides of the road. Big Al wasn't sure what to look for, but they searched.

Then, he saw it—something shiny caught his eye. They got off their bikes and walked down the embankment, and under a bunch of branches—quite a few branches—they found Mike's bike. It wasn't his original bike, but the one he had traded for.

"Gotcha," said Big Al. "That bastard survived that beating. I don't bloody believe it. He didn't take his bike though. I wonder where he went or if he's still alive."

The others just stood there and didn't answer. They figured Mike was dead and wondered why Big Al was bothering with all of this. He told them to recover the bike and made arrangements for one of them to return to the spot with another rider and take the bike away. The key was still in it, and it looked like it could still run.

This was not Mike's real bike. It was the bike he took off on when they found him. Big Al thought that Mikey wouldn't be hard to find. He felt that Mike's original one-of-a-kind Harley was the key to finding the traitor.

He wanted Mike to pay for his pain, his betrayal, and Charley's death. For weeks, there were no reports of his bike being seen anywhere. His bike would easily stand out. It was a custom design that Mike had put together expertly. The gang was missing Mikey because he was a great mechanic. He was fast, and he was good. He could fix anything and could redesign a motorcycle into a beautiful one-of-a-kind machine. He had put together a one-of-a-kind bike. The handles were long and high. The chrome on the bike was magnificent. An extra-long seat with extra padding was wrapped in red leather. The rest of the bike was black and chrome, so the red leather seat stood out. There was no mistaking Mike Ryan's bike for anyone else's. It also had two large compartments on either side of the seat for supplies.

The gang got a lucky breakthrough when word was going around that some bike shop near Cincinnati was selling a one-of-a-kind bike. From the description, it sounded like Mike's bike. The clincher was the red seat. Who else would have a red seat? So Big Al and a few friends set off to the bike shop. When they got there, there was no doubt it was Mike's bike. Now they had to figure out how to find him.

The owner of the shop didn't take too long to break. It only took two hits to the stomach and two punches to the face for him to tell them what Mike was now riding. They figured he wasn't lying about not knowing where Mike was headed. Mike wasn't that stupid. The owner told them which way he had headed out of town, and they started their search in the direction of Cincinnati.

Where does a biker go without a bike? thought Big Al. *And how in the hell did he walk away from that beating? I will find you, Mikey, make no doubt about that.*

Chapter 15

March 2004

After leaving with his new motorcycle, Mike had to figure out how he would make ends meet. The money he had collected would not last long, so he had to make decisions fast. Mike did not know how to do many things. He had finished high school, but he was not trained for any job. He had learned about bikes as time went on. He was a quick study. He had an uncanny ability to take apart a motorcycle and put it together exactly the way it started or put it together the way he wanted. So the only way he could support himself was to find a job at a bike shop. He didn't want to look like he knew too much, however. He wanted to blend in and not stand out. He didn't want people to talk about him. There was a slight chance that Big Al had survived the gunshot. Any possibility of this meant trouble for Mike. He had to make sure that the fact that he was still alive did not get back to the Mid Town Boys, and more specifically, to Big Al. If Big Al had any inkling that Mike was alive, Mike knew that he would be hunted down.

He found a small bike shop that had recently let go of one of their mechanics. He convinced the owner that he knew a little about bikes. Summer was coming, and it was the beginning of the shop's busy season, so the owner hired Mike. Mike even found himself some living quarters, above the shop. He could just roll out of bed, go to work, and then walk quietly upstairs to bed. He worked long hours and loved it. At night, he sat and thought about what he was going to do with the rest of his life. *Is this all I want?* he thought.

Life went on for one month or so. Joe, the owner of Joe's Bike Shop, was delighted with Mike. He didn't mind working overtime, and Joe had come to realize that Mike really did know what he was doing. People started to spread the word about the mechanic at Joe's and that the mechanic was good and fast. Unfortunately, the word spread a little too far.

Chapter 16

May 2, 2004

One of the Mid Town Boys had a breakdown just outside of Cincinnati. The tow truck driver that came to pick him up and take him to a garage said that there was a crack of a mechanic at Joe's Bike Shop. He suggested that they take the bike there. So the guy agreed. The bike was fixed in record time and was running even better than it was before it broke down. The gang member rode away with a big smile.

When he got to the safe house, he told the boys how his bike had broken down, and this guy fixed it in record time. He bragged about how much more power he felt in his machine. No one seemed to really care, except for Big Al.

"What did the guy look like?" he asked.

"Average, I guess. He looked like a biker, if we look like anything. Long hair, beard, jeans, you know." This biker had never met Mike as he was a new recruit to the Mid Town Boys.

"Did you find out his name?"

"No, now that you mention it, no one mentioned his name. They kept on saying, 'Hey, mechanic.'"

"Anything special about the guy?"

"Naw. Hey, what's so special about his guy anyway?"

"Just wondering. We had a great mechanic here once, and he left. I thought, Jesus, if that was him, then maybe we could convince to come back. Our bikes could use some tuning up."

This guy didn't know it, but Big Al's reputation in the bike world had diminished tremendously after he had been shot in the struggle with Mike and Mike had gotten away. He had to seek revenge against Mike for not completing the hit on Los Alamos and leaving Big Al to die. It was important that everyone knew that, so no one would even think of committing such a violation of gang codes again.

"I don't know about that. It didn't look like he would leave that place. The owner loved him. The guy was really quiet. He didn't even look me in the eyes. I just figured he was one of those shy and quiet types, ya know?"

"Yeah, yeah. You're probably right."

"I did notice one thing," he added. "He had this tattoo on his left arm. I thought it was great."

Big Al was interested now. Mike had had a tattoo put on his arm when he first came to the gang. It was a funny tattoo for a man to get; it was a broken heart. What kind of man puts a broken heart on his arm? Why would you want people to know you'd had your heart broken? Everyone had made fun of him at the time. Mike didn't care what anyone thought about his tattoo though. It was what it was.

"A big red heart with those jagged edges on it."

Bingo, that's him, Big Al thought. "Where's this place?" he asked the biker.

"It's called Joe's Place, just on the west side of Cincinnati. It's not very big."

He gave Big Al his receipt for the mechanical work. It had the address and phone number on it. Big Al smiled. *I've got the chicken shit,* he thought. *Now he's going to pay for being a traitor. No one does something like this to me and gets away with it.*

The next morning, Big Al and about ten gang members headed out for Cincinnati. They had no trouble finding the place. They parked their bikes in some trees away from the shop and stood across the street waiting for sight of "the mechanic." A tow truck showed up with another broken-down motorcycle. The tow truck driver went into the shop, and when he came back out, Mike was walking beside him. Big Al couldn't believe it. There he was in plain sight. The others wanted to go and get him right away, but Big Al said, "We'll wait till he's alone."

At the end of the workday, Joe left his shop in Mike's capable hands. He knew Mike would keep working on the bike that just came in until he was satisfied that he had fixed it. Mike was happy because he felt at peace when he worked by himself—no interruptions, no phone calls, just work. He decided to go upstairs to his loft to make a quick snack.

Joe had been gone for about fifteen minutes when Big Al and his pals walked across the street. Big Al was excited now. Preparing to kill someone always excited him.

Mike heard glass break and the sound of people entering the garage. He figured someone was breaking into Joe's shop, and he was not about to get involved. *It sounds like there are a lot of them,* he thought. *I'm staying put.*

Then Mike's heart practically stopped beating. He heard a voice he knew—Big Al. *Damn, how the hell did he find me?* Mike had to get the hell out of there because they would eventually notice the staircase. He opened the small window that led to an old fire escape. He crawled out and quietly went down the stairs. No one heard him until he started his bike.

"He's getting away!" yelled Big Al. "Get your bikes."

Mike took off away from town. He got on the highway and headed north. He had increased the power of his new bike, and now it could really move. However, he knew that Big Al and the others also had powerful bikes. He knew because he had practically built every bike. Mike had to go faster than any other time in his life. He knew that if they caught him, he was dead.

They guessed right when they got to the highway. They also headed north. Two bikers had gone south, just in case. They rode as fast as they could. Big Al was not going to give up. They saw a bike about a half a mile ahead of them. "I think that's him!" Big Al yelled to the others. That spurred them on to go even faster.

Mike heard the bikes and knew he had to get off the highway and see if he could lose them on the country roads. Maybe he could find a place to hide. He took the next exit and headed into cottage country. The roads were tree lined and had many curves and hills. *Maybe, I can outride them,* he thought.

Unfortunately, the bikers Big Al had assembled were accomplished riders and had no trouble catching up to Mike. The replacement bike had been improved upon, but it was not his old Harley. It was just a matter of Al and the boys encircling him and riding him off the road.

Mike knew the jig was up. He couldn't go anywhere. There were bikes in front of him, behind him, and beside him. He turned to his left and saw Big Al smiling at him.

Big Al steered his bike to the right and knocked Mike and his bike onto the side of the road. Mike went sideways, lost his balance on the gravel, and fell off his bike. *Shit,* he thought, *I'm dead now.*

Chapter 17

April 14, 2004

The reviews were fantastic. The ballet world had a new diva and a new duo. Peter Rogers was now paired with Elizabeth Hamilton. Both received outstanding reviews, but everyone was focused on Elizabeth. It wasn't that she was unknown or a flash in the pan. She was just a quiet dancer who wasn't seen much around town. She avoided the press and paparazzi. They wanted to know more about her and more about her relationship with her partner. It was what great stories were made of—beautiful dancer in love with her partner.

"We're getting some great reviews," said Peter as they were changing after a performance.

They shared a large dressing room now. They were a couple on the stage and in their lives.

"Yes," replied Elizabeth. "I'm so glad. I don't want to be a disappointment for the Company."

"Babe, you could never be a disappointment to the Company. You *are* the Company. Don't you realize that people are coming to see Elizabeth Hamilton?"

Elizabeth looked at him with cynicism. She did not trust the accolades of the public.

"Everyone's also coming to see you. You're the principal male dancer of this production, don't forget. I could not dance as I do without you beside me."

Peter smiled. He loved her more than he could say. She was so humble and modest. She did not realize how great of a dancer she was.

"Yeah, as long as I'm lifting you up and down and following you around the stage."

"Peter, really?"

He dropped the subject and continued dressing. She would not bend on this point, so it was just better to drop it. Peter knew that he was an accomplished dancer, but he also knew that his success would not have been so timely, if he hadn't been lucky in getting Elizabeth as a partner.

People were flocking to the theatre to see the ballet itself and the love story between these two dancers unfold on stage. He lifted her with such care and love. She flew through the air and landed in his arms gracefully. She had complete trust in him on the stage and in life. She knew that Peter loved her. He made her feel special, and their romance was speeding forward. But . . .

It was going too fast for Elizabeth. Two weeks after the opening of the ballet, she was not sleeping very well. She tossed and turned all night, even when she managed to spend the night with Peter.

"I cannot wait until we can go home together and stay together all night," Peter said.

"Me too. But I'm not ready to leave my mother alone in our condo. Too many memories, and I don't want her to feel lonely. I'm not sure you moving in there would be a good idea," Elizabeth replied.

"I don't want to move into your condo with you and your mother. I want us to move into *our* place. I'll wait until the sale goes through and we find our own place."

Elizabeth did not have the courage to leave her mother alone and move in with Peter, or to have Peter move in with them. Her mother probably would have accepted the arrangement, but something was holding Elizabeth back. *Why am I holding back?* she asked herself constantly. *I should be living every moment of my life and not questioning everything. What's wrong with me?*

These thoughts were in her mind during sleep, during rehearsals, and during performances. She couldn't shake them.

Peter, on the other hand, was ecstatic about his life. He was living his dream. He was dancing—and dancing very well. He was receiving rave reviews from all over the world. And best of all, he was partnered with the most beautiful girl in the world, and they loved each other. He was hoping that Monique would move into a new place by herself, and Elizabeth could move in with him. Or better yet, they could get married. He knew he still had to go slowly. He could see fear in Elizabeth's eyes every now and then and wondered why.

Monique called Elizabeth at the rehearsal studio and asked her to meet her at an apartment building not far from the studio.

Peter decided to join Elizabeth.

"Your mom seems to be excited about moving."

"Yes. I'm a little surprised because we have lived in that apartment my entire life, and she seems to be anxious to leave it.

Elizabeth and Peter headed off to the apartment building where Monique was waiting for them beside a business-looking woman.

"This is Jane Miller, a realtor," she said.

"Oh, nice to meet you," said Elizabeth.

Everyone shook hands. Monique looked excited.

"What's up, Mom?" said Elizabeth. "You look like you're ready to jump out of your pants."

"I am rather excited," she said. "I think I've found the perfect apartment."

"Oh," said Elizabeth in surprise. "I didn't realize you were looking behind my back."

"Oh, don't be silly, dear. I simply arranged time to visit a few places with Jane. I knew that you didn't have the time right now to go house hunting."

"Well, everyone, shall we go up?" asked Jane.

"Yes, let's," said Monique.

Elizabeth was scared. She didn't know why she had such a big knot in her stomach entering the building. What could possibly have her so stressed out viewing a condo?

It was beautiful—close to the dance studio, the dance hall, and Monique's office. There were two bedrooms with their own ensuite washrooms. The kitchen was huge (not that it would be used much). There was a balcony with a to-die-for view. Central Park was quite amazing at this height. The spring flowers were starting to bloom, and the trees were beginning to bud.

"Can you imagine standing on this balcony and watching the seasons change?" Monique whispered to Elizabeth.

Elizabeth nodded.

It was on the twenty-seventh floor, so there was no noise from the streets below. Monique loved the fact that there was a big, welcoming foyer. She also loved the architectural touches—the crown moldings, the medallions on the ceiling, the woodwork in the family room, the built-in storage in all the rooms. Monique had found what she felt was *the* place.

"What do you think, honey?" she asked Elizabeth.

"It's beautiful, Mom. Are you sure that you're ready to leave our place? We've never lived anywhere else. At least, I haven't lived anywhere else. Are you sure?"

"Yes," said Monique. "I think it's perfect. There are two bedrooms with their own ensuites and plenty of room for the three of us."

"The three of us?"

"Yes, honey, the three of us."

Everyone stopped walking. They had left Jane and told her that they would call her with their decision. They were walking toward their favorite restaurant for dinner. Peter couldn't believe what he was hearing. Elizabeth froze.

"I think it's time for the two of you to have a real relationship. I've been thinking about this for some time now. I don't mean to stick my nose in your business, but I'm a mother."

"Mom," stuttered Elizabeth.

"No, no, don't stop me now. Here it is. I would love it if the two of you would move in with me. However, I don't need that to happen. I would be happy if the two of you got your own place. I just want you to know that the choice is there for the two of you to make. There will always be a bedroom at my home for the two of you, for visits. Or if you want to move in with me, so be it. I think we get along just fine, and this would also please me. Nevertheless, this would be entirely up to the two of you. Now, I made arrangements with a friend for dinner. So we will sit at our table, and the two of you can discuss the choices."

On that note, Monique waved to her friend, who was already seated. The maître d' knew Elizabeth and Peter well and escorted them to their own table.

They sat in silence until the waiter came for their drink orders. Both of them ordered cocktails, which was odd since they were performing the next day. They felt like they needed one. They stared at the menus until the drinks came. Asking for more time, they dismissed the waiter.

Peter started the conversation. "Shall we have a toast to our future?"

Elizabeth looked at him. His eyes were shining, and she knew what he was thinking. He wanted them to be together.

He may even want to get married, she thought, *and why is that bothering me?*

"Yes, let's toast that we make the right choice for our future."

"I stand corrected; to the right choice."

Their glasses clinked, and Peter took her hand in his and kissed it. *He is really sweet,* she thought.

"I guess your mother has forced our hand. Liz, you know how I feel. You know that any one of these choices would please me. I would prefer to have our own place, but if you want to live with your mom, then that's fine with me. I'll even make an honest woman of you, if you'd like."

Elizabeth knew it. She knew that's what he was thinking. *What do I do now?* she thought.

"Peter, I'm not sure if I'm ready to be so open in front of my mother."

"Oh, Liz, get over it. Do you really think your mother doesn't know we've been having sex? She's not that stupid or naive. She's a modern woman, Liz, and she wants you to be happy. Really, babe, just get that thought out of your mind and enjoy your life."

Elizabeth was feeling cornered. She didn't like either of the choices. The third alternative—just moving into the new apartment with her mother, without Peter—had not been mentioned. Monique and Peter had decided that there were only two choices. She was panicking and didn't understand why.

She looked at Peter. *Why am I not jumping at this? He's gorgeous—blond hair, green eyes, great ass, great dancer, and he loves me. What's wrong with me?*

She didn't like where this was going, and it was going way too fast in her opinion. But she felt like she didn't have a choice. She would, however, pick the one that was the least frightening. She was not ready to get married, and she didn't know why. Nevertheless, she would delay that step, at least.

"Peter, I'm not ready to leave my mother alone. I think we could postpone thoughts of a marriage and move in with her in this new place. How do you feel about that"?

With that, Peter jumped up in joy. He grabbed Elizabeth and pulled her off her seat. He gave her a huge hug and an even bigger kiss. He then rushed over to where Monique was sitting and told Monique what Elizabeth had said. Monique screamed with joy and hugged Peter. She then blew a kiss to Elizabeth. Elizabeth waved back. Peter ran back to Liz, kissed her again, and sat down, gleaming at her.

Elizabeth smiled too. On the inside, however, she was shaking. She should be delighted and excited, but all she felt was dread. *One step at a time, Elizabeth,* she said to herself. *One step at a time.*

Chapter 18

July 2004

Ten weeks flew by. Mike was stiff from not moving too much, but he didn't feel any more pain in his chest and stomach. His eyes had healed, but the skin around his right eye sported a nice scar.

Elizabeth had danced every morning from 9:00 to 11:00. She wanted to keep her body in shape, and it was also important for her to keep her stress level down. The deck had been designed with a top bar all around the railing. It was the perfect ballet height so that Elizabeth could practice and dance while at the cottage. There was a sound system set up so that she could play whatever music she needed at any time. She had been tossing and turning at night lately, and she thought it was from inactivity. She was also starting to feel guilty about Peter and wondering how he was dealing with her sudden departure.

She was calling her mother from town and reassuring her that all was okay. Last week, she had told her where she had been staying. She didn't like deceiving her. Monique was relieved when she heard where Elizabeth had gone. She knew that she must have been feeling much inner pain to have left so suddenly, and her mother felt good that she went to the cottage for solace.

Peter had moved out of her apartment one month after Elizabeth left. He was distraught. He continued the ballet, however, and had gotten used to his new partner. Their reviews were very good—not as good as when Elizabeth was dancing, but very good. He couldn't bear to go to Monique's apartment, and after two weeks, he started to look for his own place again. He was still holding onto hope of finding her. He knew that Monique must have been contacted because she didn't have the whole police force looking for her daughter, but he was also pretty sure that she didn't know where Elizabeth had gone.

"Have you heard from Elizabeth at all?" Peter asked Monique.

"No, dear. I'm just hoping that she's okay. I don't know why she would leave so unexpectedly like this." Monique did not want to break any confidence between her and her daughter. Elizabeth wanted and needed to be alone right now, so Monique respected her wishes. She felt sorry for Peter because he was clearly devastated by the circumstances.

"I'll call you in a few days then." He knew that Monique had to have had contact with Elizabeth—they were too close. But he didn't want to push Monique too hard.

He woke up, went to rehearsal, had lunch, had a nap, went to the auditorium, danced, came home, and went to bed. He was performing all his duties by rote. He was missing Elizabeth's softness and her smile. He felt half-whole.

Chapter 19

July 2004

Big Al had healed completely. He was still the big-ass boss of the Mid Town Boys. He had taken care of Mikey, and the word had spread through the biker world. No one wanted to cross Big Al. However, Big Al had not forgotten the betrayal. He had protected Mikey and brought him up the ranks of the gang, and what did he get? A kick in the head. He would not forget that.

Life had changed for Mike. He was no longer on edge and no longer worried about what new adventure the Mid Town Boys would concoct. He found himself thinking positively about himself for the first time in years.

Michael Ryan would watch her every morning going through her dancing routine. He had grown to love the music she played. He would sit with his coffee on the dock and watch her. If he tilted his hat just so, it seemed like he was taking a nap. But all the while, he watched every move Elizabeth was making. He did not like the fact that he was hooked on this daily ritual. *I have to start thinking about leaving this place,* he thought. *I'm getting way too used to this. This is no good for me and for her. She deserves much more than me.*

Elizabeth was wondering when the day would come when Michael Ryan would disappear from the cottage. She chastised herself for wishing that he would stay. She still loved Peter, didn't she? She was now a regular in town, and people were now saying hello to her when she went in for supplies. *I could get used to living out here,* she thought. But she had started missing the dance. She wanted to feel that utter exhaustion one feels at the end of a hard rehearsal. She had always enjoyed that feeling. But she also enjoyed the feeling she received when she returned to the cottage. Michael Ryan would be waiting for her, sitting on the dock or sitting on the deck. He had managed a pretty good tan the last few weeks. She had managed to get him to keep his beard off of his face, but he still sported a ponytail. He did not let his hair down anymore, but he didn't want to cut it.

"I've been wondering," said Mike, "how we could find out if my bike is still on the side of that road."

"I'm sure it is. I covered with a great deal of branches and leaves."

"Yeah, yeah, that's what you said. I'm thinking that it's time to see then if it works—if it's still there, that is."

"Well, we could go to the spot. I'm sure I could find it."

"I'm still not good with that. I don't want you more involved than you are already. I still don't trust those guys. They're not the type of guys to give up on anything. You don't understand bikers; they would definitely come after me if they knew I was alive."

Elizabeth did not want to see those men again. She had seen the smiles on their faces as they were passing her car. They were smiling after they had just, what they thought, killed someone. Those were not the kind of people she wanted to bump into.

"Do you really need that bike?" Elizabeth asked.

"I have nothing here. There was some money in the pouch on the side of the bike. That's all I had in this world. And I need wheels. How the hell am I supposed to get along? I can't stay here much longer. I have to start taking care of myself."

She understood how he was feeling, but she didn't want him to leave, did she? It was still a question in her mind as to why she was attracted to Michael Ryan. He was not the type of person she would have socialized with in New York. He was at the opposite end of that spectrum. But there was something about him that drew her toward him. She could not explain it. It was a feeling and a flutter when she was near him.

"Is it possible to have a tow truck pick it up? It may not be a good idea. They might find that money. Maybe we should just check out the bike and see if it's worth retrieving."

"That's true. We'd have to go at night and make absolutely sure no one saw us. If those guys get any clue that I'm alive, I will definitely be dead. They don't screw up twice. I'm not sure that you should go with me."

"Do you know the location of the bike?"

"I'll figure it out. Like I already said, it's better than getting you involved again."

"I'm already involved, and you have no way of knowing where that bike is. If I do say so myself, I did a pretty good job hiding it. When would you like to go? I measured the distance with my odometer, so it shouldn't take us long to find the spot."

Odometer—she's smarter than I thought. Who the hell does something like that?

"Well, waste not, want not. Let's go tonight."

"Tonight?"

"Yeah, why not? We can check out the bike and then decide how we're going get it here. If we can get it here, I can fix it. I know I can."

So they had a plan.

They both felt good about having a plan. Elizabeth had started to become a little bored, and this gave her something to look forward to. She also liked the idea of doing something with Mr. Ryan. Mike was going stir crazy, so he would have gone anywhere for a change of pace. And he too liked the idea of doing something with Miss Hamilton.

He slept a little better that night. He had something to do, and he felt a little more alive just thinking about it.

Elizabeth was glad about the plan, but she was worried about going near that motorcycle. She thought it would cause problems.

They were both in their separate beds, lying awake and doing lots of thinking. They fell asleep thinking about what the future would bring.

Chapter 20

Late July 2004

It was a perfect night to look for something in the dark. It was a full moon, and in the country, the moon illuminated a huge area of space. You could have driven with your lights off and still have been able to see the road.

Elizabeth had her headlights on, however. She was looking for the landmark of the tree. She had noticed the tree that night and had thought that it looked like it had been hit with lightning. It was blackened and bent over. So when the odometer signaled that they had traveled the required number of miles, she started looking to her right for the tree. She knew this would mean that to her left, under leaves, should be the bike.

"We're just about there," said Elizabeth.

"How do you know?"

"The odometer reading is hitting the right number of miles—the same as that night."

"Okay."

"Look!" she exclaimed. "There's the tree—the lightning tree."

"What?"

"The tree, the tree I saw that night. We should stop here and start walking on the other side of the road."

"Okay, but we have to move fast. I don't want anyone to see your car or us. This is not right. I don't like this."

"Well, we must get out if you want to find your motorcycle."

Elizabeth quickly pulled over. She went as far off the road as she could. They ran across the street and started looking through the bush. There was nothing on the road or the gravel to indicate that there had been an incident.

Mike had quickly gone down the bank and was swinging his hands to try to feel something.

"Are you sure about the spot?" he hollered.

"Yes, yes, I'm positive. If we don't find it, then someone took it."

That's a thought Mike didn't want to consider. He needed that bike. He hoped with all his might that he would find the stupid bike. He didn't even like it that much, but it served its purpose. He was just about ready to give up when his foot hit something. He started swinging his arms lower into the branches, and he hit something hard. It was his bike. He couldn't believe it. She had pinpointed the location, and he was amazed.

"It's here," he yelled.

"Pardon?"

"I found it."

"Thank God." With that statement, Elizabeth ran down the embankment as well and helped Mike remove the branches.

"Jesus, you certainly did cover it, didn't you."

"I didn't want anyone to see your motorcycle. You told me they would kill you if they came back. I believed you. I think my fear made me move at super speed that night."

She could laugh about it now, but just remembering that night raised Elizabeth's heart rate, and she had to admit to herself that she was scared right now.

Mike found his money pouch, and to his surprise, the money was still there. It had been rained on and all stuck together, but it was still there.

"Okay, let's get the hell outta here," Mike said.

He grabbed Elizabeth's arm and pulled her back up the embankment. He obviously was getting his strength back because it was a swift and smooth movement up to the road. They ran to the car and drove away. Elizabeth, again, reset the odometer.

Elizabeth phoned her auto club early the next morning and told them to pick up the bike from the side of the road. She told them the location and that she would be waiting for the tow truck. Mike didn't like it. He was not happy about being out in the open dealing with this bike. "What if the tow truck driver mentions it to someone?" They had decided that she would go alone and tell the driver that her brother had lost control and went off the road. He was back home still drunk and asked his sister to hide the bike and get it back home before his parents would find out. Mike told her to tell the story and go on and on about it, even if it looked like they didn't care or weren't listening. "Drill it into their minds," he said.

The tow truck arrived about fifteen minutes later than expected. Those extra minutes had seemed like fifteen hours to Elizabeth. Michael had scared her to death about the whole thing. She, of course, didn't understand how dangerous the gang members were. However, he did.

Two men had come to retrieve the bike. They were glad there were two of them. It was hard getting that damn bike up that embankment. And the woman wouldn't shut up about her brother. She was more of a bother than the stupid bike. They were glad to get in their truck so that they wouldn't hear her chatter about her brother and her parents—stupid kids, drinking and riding bikes. The kid was lucky he was just hung over and not dead.

Elizabeth turned her car around, and the tow truck followed her around the bend.

Just as the tow truck was rounding the bend, the driver noticed three huge bikes coming up the road behind him. Then the truck went around the corner. The bikes did not follow.

Chapter 21

July 2004

Big Al had been bothered by the fact that there had been no stories about a biker being found dead on the side of a country road near Cincinnati. *Why not? People love stories about bikers. They love to hate us,* he thought.

He decided to go back to the scene of the crime and check it out. He wanted to see a body or something that would prove to him that Mikey was dead.

I'll just take a few guys with me, he thought. *I'll tell them that I'm just looking for a spot for a new house. Yeah, I'll say that we're gonna be moving.*

He figured that he could find the spot where they had caught up to Mikey. He remembered the turn off from the highway. He remembered that he thought, at the time, *Where the hell is he heading?* So he left with three other riders for what he called the country.

"Why're we goin' into the country, Al?" one of the riders asked. "Are we all movin' out here?"

"I don't know," answered Al. "Just ride, for Chrissakes. Just ride."

"Yeah, yeah, right, Al. Just wonderin', that's all."

Big Al wasn't sure why this whole thing was nagging at him. He had taken care of the traitor, and everyone in the gang had learned a lesson about crossing him. Of that, he was sure. But he wanted some kind of evidence that proved to him that the problem had been solved and would not return.

He got them to slow down around where he thought they had cornered Mikey. None of the three guys that went with him was there that night. Nothing about the location would tip them off. They wouldn't have a clue that he was looking for proof that Mikey was indeed dead. He had received a lot of praise for knocking off a traitor, so he didn't want people to consider that he hadn't carried through with his punishment.

"I think one of the guys lost a gun in this area a while back," Big Al shouted to the other bikers.

"What do you want us to do?"

"Take a look around and see if you see anything."

So everyone got off their motorcycles and started walking up and down the side of the road.

They were on the right stretch of road, but they were not going down into the ditch low enough to find Mike's bike.

Elizabeth had done a very good job covering it. It had taken away time from dealing with Michael's injuries, but it obviously was time well spent.

Kicking and shaking their feet through the dirt did not produce a gun.

So, where did the bike go? he thought. *It had to go somewhere, and how did it get there?*

Big Al was left wondering where Mike's body would have ended up. He wanted proof that he had taken care of the traitor. All this proved is that Mike had disappeared somehow, and so had his bike.

This meant there were things left open. He had not been able to close the book on Mike Ryan, and he was pissed.

Chapter 22

Now it was Elizabeth's turn to watch. She had not seen such a gleam in Michael Ryan's eyes. She saw it as he worked on that motorcycle. It was a joy to behold. It seemed that life had reentered his body. He had come alive.

He gave her money and a list of tools that he would need to repair the bike. He looked like a little boy receiving a new toy when she arrived. He took great care in carrying the tools into the shed. He had a look of peace and excitement as he started his work.

His endurance wasn't what it used to be. After a few hours of very slow work, Mike was exhausted. He came into the cottage covered in dirt and oil. Elizabeth had just finished dancing, and she was wiping her face with her towel. They looked at each other and started to laugh. They both had sweat pouring down their faces. He was covered with oil, and she was covered with glistening body oils.

Their eyes caught each other for a brief moment, and both man and woman turned away.

"Well, I'll be jumping in the shower," said Mike.

"Okay, you go first, and I'll rustle up some lunch."

"Sounds good," he said.

Shit, I could have jumped her. Christ, how can someone look so good while they're sweating that much. No, no, that wasn't sweat. She was shining. I haven't seen anything that good in weeks. Shit, I've never seen anything that good, period.

Mike ran a cool shower, and it felt good. He was starting to feel the strain on his body from all that physical work. It had been a long time—way too long. *I have to stop thinking about her like this. She's in a different class. She's just helping me out, and she doesn't think about me like this at all.* He tried not to think of Elizabeth but couldn't stop.

He finished up and dried himself off. He walked out of the washroom with a towel around his waist and was shaking out his hair to attempt to dry it a bit. He had shaved his face, and he truly looked great. At least, he did to Elizabeth. She inhaled when she turned to look in the direction of the washroom.

Wow, he's got a great body. It still shows signs of being beaten up, but it looks good. And even that stupid long hair looks good today. What am I thinking?

Elizabeth finished up the preparations for lunch. She was trying to make herself focus on the food.

"Your turn," Mike announced.

"Oh, oh, thanks," said Elizabeth. "I'll just hop into the shower, and then I'll get lunch out."

"No rush," said Mike. "Take your time and enjoy your shower."

Elizabeth wiped her hands and headed off to the shower.

Mike had changed and was sitting having a beer at the kitchen table when Elizabeth came out of the washroom. She, too, came out with a towel wrapped around her body. Mike just about dropped his beer. *Jesus,* he thought. She came out quickly, carrying her clothes and holding up her towel. *Oh, I wish it would fall,* he admitted to himself.

Elizabeth didn't look up. She was trying to get upstairs to her room as quickly as possible, without being seen. She had not thought of bringing her clothes down before she entered the shower. She was upset about herself for that. *I don't need to go walking around here half-naked.*

Elizabeth returned to the kitchen a few minutes later. It seemed like hours to Mike. He was still dreaming about the towel falling off. The beer felt good, and his body was melting. His muscles were sore, and he enjoyed it. Elizabeth got out the lunch in no time and presented sandwiches and fruit on the kitchen table. She poured herself a glass of lemonade, and they, again, sat in silence and ate their food.

They were both focused on their own thoughts—on each other.

Chapter 23

He had learned the name of her favorite piece of music—Beethoven's *Moonlight Sonata*. She danced to that song more often than to any other. He could even hum the song to himself now. He had heard it almost every day for weeks.

They had moved into a very enjoyable daily routine: early rising (something Mike had never done in his life); a swim to the island and back; separate showers (something he would have loved to change); breakfast; he went to the shed to work on his bike, and she went to the deck to dance; lunch; more work on the bike for him, and reading, gardening, or supply buying for her; dinner; sitting and listening to the sounds of the lake; and then bed—separately.

It seemed almost natural for life to continue on this path. Neither one would admit it out loud.

Mike had learned to love her music. He could see her move in his mind, even though he was fixing his bike. The bike was going to end up in even better shape than it was before that night. He was even going to change the color of the bike so that no one would recognize it. It was going to be ready soon, and he was getting himself prepared mentally to leave this place.

Elizabeth had already started getting the itch to dance with a partner in a real, long, and tiring ballet. She was getting her desire and her love back for ballet. She had thought she had lost it forever, but now she felt at peace with herself and life. Thoughts of Peter flitted in and out of her mind. These thoughts, however, were being overrun by thoughts of Michael Ryan. She believed that she loved Peter, but she was developing a passion for Mr. Ryan, a passion she was trying hard to suppress.

There was obvious tension in the cottage, on the deck, on the dock, or wherever they were together. There was some sort of force drawing them closer and closer, without a word or a movement being made to encourage this closeness.

Mike would steal looks at Elizabeth on the deck dancing. He would position his body on one side of the motorcycle so that he could watch her and still make it look like he was fixing the bike.

Elizabeth would put her leg up on the bar and lean forward with her head turned so that she could watch Michael working on his bike.

They managed to get through their showers without acting on their impulses to drop their towel or tear off the other's towel. Dinnertime was sometimes painfully quiet. The sexual tension would actually come between them as they sat on the deck having meals. They would not speak then. One of them would have to break the silence and start talking about the bike, or the music, or the lake—just about anything to change the vibe at the table.

She had saved his life. He had fought hard to live. She had taken care of him, as no one had his entire life. He had allowed her to be in charge and to be herself. She had asked no questions and had trusted him completely. He had asked no questions and had trusted her to the best of his ability (she knew that this was not something he could do easily).

Elizabeth now sported a beautiful tan to go with her long and lean body. Her blonde hair gleamed against her tawny skin. Mike still wore his ponytail, but he was always clean-shaven these days, and he now had a more muscular and tanned body. He walked around bare-chested and in jeans all day, and she floated around in a bikini top and shorts. They tried not to look at each other, but when the other person was turned around, they looked, and they enjoyed what they saw.

They both knew that they were coming to a fork in the road and that it looked like one would take the road to the left and one would take the road to the right. They were both trying to figure out which road they would be taking and why this situation even bothered them.

Chapter 24

September 2004

Peter was glad that the current ballet production was ending. It had been an enormous success, even without Elizabeth. Her understudy had come in and done an excellent job of picking up where Elizabeth had left off. However, Peter wanted Elizabeth.

He was determined to find her and determined to find out why she left. He had to get the answer to why she left because he did not understand how someone could leave a production and a relationship without warning.

They had barely lived in the new condo with Monique. Feeling uncomfortable sleeping with a man at her mother's home plagued Elizabeth.

He knew that Monique had been in touch with her, and when he was finished the next Saturday night, he would begin his quest to find Elizabeth. He would then have the time to devote to this mystery.

Monique was glad that the ballet production was ending because it was a constant reminder that Elizabeth was not around. She missed her daughter. She missed her company and had always considered Elizabeth her best friend.

Monique, much to her own surprise, had begun seeing a gentleman. He was a fashion editor for a French magazine. They met on her August trip to Europe and discovered that they had many things in common, including being single parents. Working hard and giving their all for their children had become a lifestyle for Jacques and Monique.

She felt at ease with him. They had each given a great deal for the benefit of their children. Monique had not been alone, however. She had Constance. Constance had supported Monique and her baby from start to finish. She would never forget the love and support she had received from her mother when she told her about her pregnancy. They had vowed that they would be together in the raising of this child, no matter what. Elizabeth had been a blessing from the day she was born. She fulfilled Monique's being.

Now Jacques was also fulfilling her being. They spoke to each other daily. Phone bills from New York to Paris were starting to add up. They would whisk away to the other city for weekend visits. He was a kind and generous man. His two children were wonderful, and they had accepted his relationship with Monique. She had not mentioned him to Elizabeth because she wanted Elizabeth to deal with her demons and return when the dealing had ended. She did not want to complicate any aspect of Elizabeth's life.

Peter had called Monique at work on the Friday before the closing of the ballet. He asked if he could visit on Sunday. He said that he wanted to talk to her about something very important. Monique had always liked Peter very much and invited him for lunch.

When Peter arrived at the door, Monique was all prepared for her guest. The table was set, and the food was ready. It had been fun preparing a meal for more than one person. She had a bottle of wine chilling, and she looked beautiful when she answered the door. They hugged, and Monique escorted Peter into the apartment.

The apartment had not changed much since he left. He looked around at familiar pieces of furniture, and he had to admit that he missed the surroundings. He reminded himself that he had to stick to his plan.

As they ate, Peter began his quest to find Elizabeth. "I know that you've been in touch with her," he said to Monique.

"Who, dear?"

"Now, Monique, let's not get too coy. I know Elizabeth would not be gone all these months without getting in touch with you. She wouldn't want to be without you, and she wouldn't want to leave you worrying all this time. I know that for sure."

"Yes, I'm sure you do."

"My point is that I need to find her. I need to know why she left. I need to understand why she left me, not just the dancing, but me. I thought we had an everlasting relationship going. She led me to believe this. I loved being with her, dancing with her, living with her, and doing anything with her. Why didn't I see the signs?"

"I don't know if Elizabeth saw the signs, dear. She hasn't said anything to me about why she left and what was bothering her. I haven't asked. She'll talk to me about this when she feels comfortable to do so. I don't think it's a good idea for me to rush this process."

"Monique, rush? She's been gone for four months now. Surely she's figured out whatever it was or is bothering her. Surely, it's time for her to come back home."

"I miss her too, Peter," she said as she took hold of his hands. "But we have to wait."

"I can't wait anymore."

"What do you mean?"

"I would like you to tell me where she is so that I can see her and talk to her myself."

"I would be breaking a confidence, Peter. And I would never break a confidence—especially one to Elizabeth."

"Damn it, Monique. Don't you know what this is doing to me? I haven't enjoyed anything since she left. I'm always trying to figure out what I did wrong—what I did to push her away."

"Peter, she did tell me that her leaving was not caused by anything that you did. She said that it was some kind of melancholy inside of her that she had to deal with."

"Melancholy, melancholy. What the hell does that mean?"

"Peter."

"I'm sorry, I'm sorry. I know it's not your fault, but I'm becoming desperate—or I feel that I am. Please tell me where she is."

"I can't. I have to respect Elizabeth's wishes."

Peter stood up quickly, said thanks for lunch, and stormed out of the apartment, slamming the door.

Monique sat and looked at the door. She was sad for Peter, but she had no intention of breaking her daughter's confidence. She needed time to get herself together, and Monique vowed to give her that time.

On his way down in the elevator, Peter made a different vow. He vowed to himself that he would find Elizabeth and get this chapter of his life settled. *I'll get someone to find her,* he thought to himself.

Chapter 25

His bike was fixed. He had already prolonged the process. He could have been finished days before.

He wished he was a successful businessman that could offer her something. An out of work, ex-biker didn't offer much to someone like Elizabeth. She was soft, cultured, beautiful, artistic, and compassionate. He had never been swept off of his feet by a woman, but now he was. He did not like the feeling, because he felt like he wasn't in control of himself. He was starting to believe that it would be better for him to leave and not be such a pansy.

She knew he was getting near completion in his quest to repair his bike and that he would be leaving soon. She had come to terms with it. This time away from the world and the ballet world was the best thing she could have done for herself. It was all Elizabeth had ever known. She had begun to question the amount of work and time she was devoting to ballet. She knew she still needed to dance but had come to the realization that it consumed too much of her life. She had to have time away from the dance. Her goal now was to find a way to put the two worlds together. She now realized that she needed both worlds. In addition, she missed her mother. Short phone calls were not enough. She wanted to discuss this new way of thinking with Monique, her best friend. She wanted to know what was going on in her mother's life as well. They only spoke of Elizabeth during their brief calls when she went into town for supplies.

The only aspect of her life she had not unraveled was Peter. She still wasn't sure why she left him so suddenly. She wondered why looking at Peter didn't make her heart thump wildly, as it did when she watched Michael fixing his bike or returning from the shower. Why did she react so physically to this man?

Elizabeth Hamilton and Michael Ryan did not talk much to each other. Elizabeth was afraid to feel the loss that she experienced when her grandmother died. She dreaded thinking about what she would feel if and when something would happen to her mother. It took all her psychological strength to keep that fear suppressed. She knew she loved Peter, but could she commit herself to him? She was afraid of that last step.

Chapter 26

Mike did not want Elizabeth to be involved in this Big Al situation. He figured he was thought of as dead, but he didn't want to take any chances. He had simply told her that it was a gang disagreement and they were getting even. She had accepted the story, but she thought that killing was such an extreme way of dealing with a "disagreement."

In the middle of the last week of August, Mike came in for lunch. As he sat down, he said, "I'm just about finished with my bike. I should be done with everything by late this afternoon. So I'm thinking that I'll be heading off tomorrow morning, and then you can get back to your normal life."

Elizabeth kept looking down at her food. *Leaving,* she thought. *I knew it was coming.*

"You're not saying much."

"Sorry, I was just finishing off a chew. Shouldn't talk with your mouth full, you know."

"Yeah, yeah, I've heard that."

"Hmm."

"So I'll finally be out of your hair."

"Really, Michael, you weren't that much trouble. I'm glad that I could help you."

Michael. Shit. I like the way she says that.

"Yeah, right."

"You'll still have to be a little careful, you know. You can't go crazy. Your body still needs a little more time to heal. You were so badly hurt. And I do think that you should get a complete check up from a doctor somewhere."

"I don't need a doctor. You did just fine."

"I tried my best."

They finished up lunch in silence, both caught in their own thoughts and feelings. They both wished that this chapter in their lives would not end. They had not figured out the ending. They had not even started the middle.

Mike finished up his repairs in the afternoon and cleaned up his tools. He could only carry a few things, so he decided to leave some stuff in the shed. Elizabeth had gone to town to buy ingredients for a special dinner. She knew Mike loved homemade hamburgers, so she got some fresh ground beef and all the fixings for a late summer barbecue.

She called her mother as well. They spoke for quite a while this time. Elizabeth told Monique that she was just about ready to go back to the city. Monique was delighted that she would see her daughter again. Monique could not wait to tell her about her new relationship. They never spoke of Peter. She had not told Elizabeth about his visit and his insistence about finding out where Elizabeth was hiding out. She had not told her that he was still hurting and in love with her. She wanted her daughter to figure out herself first and then deal with Peter. Peter was secondary.

It was not a very nice going away barbecue. The food was delicious. Mike ate two huge hamburgers and inhaled the potato salad. Elizabeth had served a beautiful bottle of wine with dinner. They sat on the deck looking out onto the lake. It was one of those nights when the air was crisp and there was no breeze. The lake looked like a sheet of glass. You could see fish jumping out of the water. Birds were swooping down to catch their dinner. The frogs were croaking, and the crickets were chirping.

Mike was trying to stop himself from jumping up, picking her up in his arms, throwing her on the bed, and making wild, passionate love to her.

She could feel his body sitting one foot away from her. There was electricity between their two arms. They were sitting, supposedly relaxed, but both bodies were taut with tension. *Should I? Shouldn't I? What if? Am I imagining things?*

Mike got up to get himself another beer and brushed against Elizabeth's arm as he raised himself out of the chair. Both felt the electricity radiate from their arm to their heart. Both hearts skipped a beat. And both man and woman ignored the desire.

On the way to the fridge, Mike thought, *I have to get the hell out of here or I'm gonna lose it. There's only so much a man can take. If I touch her again, I won't be able to stop myself.*

I cannot cry, she thought. *I have never felt like this. I wanted to be with Peter, but not like this. What kind of feeling is this? Oh, shut up and wake up. Don't complicate matters. I'll forget about him when he leaves. Just ignore, just ignore."*

She didn't ignore very well, because Elizabeth cried herself to sleep in the loft. It was a great big bed, and she felt so alone in it. She tried to rationalize by telling herself that it was because she had not been in contact with anyone for almost four months. She told herself that as soon as he left and she returned to the city, all thoughts of Michael Ryan would disappear. However, why was she crying?

Michael Ryan wasn't crying, but he wasn't sleeping either. He tossed and turned until about four. He finally gave up, grabbed a beer, and sat on the deck looking out into the darkness. The moon was shining brightly, and there were a million stars in the sky. The normal night noises were around, and he had grown to enjoy those sounds. He was trying to get himself to relax. *This is the perfect place to relax. Why the hell can't I just sit and think of nothing? Because she' up there. She's lying in bed, maybe naked (he felt himself stir), and I'm down here looking at a freakin' lake. What the hell's with that?*

Elizabeth woke up at seven. She had not had a good night. She rose quietly and decided to have a shower. Her eyes were swollen, and she felt like crap. When she came down the stairs, she saw that Michael was not in the bed. *Oh my God*, she thought. *Did he leave without saying good-bye?* But then she saw him sitting on the deck. Big breath.

When she came out of the shower, Mike was making her grandmother's bed for the last time. Elizabeth held onto her towel, bowed her head, and slipped back upstairs.

Jesus, I've got to get outta here.

"Good morning," she said as she returned downstairs.

"Good morning."

"It's another beautiful day. Some of the trees are starting to turn color. It's going to be beautiful around here in about four or five weeks."

Mike didn't reply. He would have liked to see those colors with her. They could swim, make love, eat, look at the colors, make love, and make love.

I have to get rid of these thoughts.

Elizabeth could hardly swallow the breakfast she had made. Mike barely got it down himself.

"Well, I packed up my things on my bike. I left some tools in the shed. I hope you don't mind."

"No, no, that's fine."

He pushed himself up from the chair and held out his hand.

Elizabeth got up. She moved toward him and put her arms around his chest. "Now, Michael Ryan, you don't think that you're going to leave here with a handshake, do you?"

He was stunned. His whole body was reacting to the touch of hers. Every contact point was causing an electrical charge in his body. He couldn't speak. He slowly, very slowly, put his arms around her shoulders.

Shit, she feels so good.

Elizabeth pulled away. "Wasn't that better than a handshake?"

"Yeah, yeah."

He took his hands and tilted her face to meet his face. They were now looking directly into each other's eyes.

His were a bright, marine blue, and hers were a soft, clear green. It took every ounce of will power he had ever had in his life to finish this the way he thought was right.

"I want you to know that what you have done for me in the last few months was more than anyone—*anyone*—has done for me my whole life. I owe you my life. You know that, don't you?"

She tried to shake her head, but he had her eyes caught in a trance.

"I will never forget my time here. This cottage will be stamped in my brain forever. I wish things were different. I wish I was different. I wish . . . I wish lots of things."

He could feel himself losing it.

"All I can say is thank you. Thank you from the bottom of my heart. You nursed me back to life. You showed me what a kind, normal human being can be, and I'm going to always keep you close to my heart."

Tears were welling in Elizabeth's eyes. She blinked. Two large alligator tears rolled down her cheeks. He wiped away one with one finger and kissed the other.

"I'll never forget you."

With that statement, Michael Ryan turned and left the cottage. Elizabeth was frozen in her spot. She heard his motorcycle start up and leave. She listened intently until she could no longer hear it. Then her shoulders drooped, her head dropped, and she allowed herself to feel the pain.

Chapter 27

October 2004

Elizabeth was changing after swimming to the island twice. It had been good therapy, but it did not fill the hole she was feeling. She felt so alone in the cottage. It was different now.

The knock on the door broke her thoughts.

He came back, she thought.

She threw on her top and raced down the stairs. Her heart was beating so quickly that she thought she was having a heart attack.

She grabbed the doorknob and threw the door open.

"Peter."

Peter Rogers was standing at the door. There were tears in his eyes, and his lips were trembling. He was carrying a huge bouquet of white roses.

Elizabeth was stunned.

"At last I found you," said Peter.

Elizabeth stood there with her mouth open and her hand still on the doorknob.

Peter could not contain himself, so he rushed forward and picked her up off the floor. He was trembling as he hugged her.

"I don't know why you left. I don't want to know, unless you want to tell me. And I don't care. All I care about is being with you. I haven't thought about anything else since you left."

She still hadn't said a word.

He put her down, put down the flowers, and took one step back to look at her. She looked great. She had a tan. He had never seen her skin tanned. Her hair had lightened from the sun, and she looked different. He couldn't put his finger on it, but her eyes were different.

"Penny for your thoughts."

"Peter."

She had to admit that it felt good when he held her. She had missed close and intimate contact. However, she was confused. It was not what she was expecting when she opened the door. But here was this man, with flowers and tears and hugs and commitment and love. She knew she needed love. Was it fate? Was it fate that he found her now? Was it right that Michael Ryan was out of her life and Peter was in? Is this what God or the angels were trying to tell her?

All these things were going through her mind at lightning speed. Then she raised herself up on her tiptoes, jumped forward, and wrapped her arms around Peter's neck. She sobbed. They sat on the porch swinging together for two hours. He kept on doling out tissue. She released four months of emotions onto Peter's shoulders.

Peter did not say a word. He was so happy that he had found her and she was safe. He had cried with her in those painful minutes, and he had cried for her.

When Peter had left Monique's apartment almost two months before, he had vowed that he would find her. He hired a private detective agency to help him in his quest. They had waited for Elizabeth to contact Monique. They had followed Monique, but she had not given them any clues to Elizabeth's location.

Finally, Elizabeth had called Monique, and they had spoken long enough for a trace to be completed. The private detective had bribed a telephone company worker to watch Monique's home and work phone and to trace all calls. One of the calls had finally paid off for them. It was from a little town outside of Cincinnati. The private detective had visited the town and asked about Elizabeth very quietly. He found out that she had been coming into town for the past few months getting supplies and then returning to the lake.

He waited for Elizabeth's next pit stop. He waited four days, and then into town she came. He watched her from his car go to the few shops in town and load up on supplies. He had a picture of her from Peter and was certain this was the woman his client was trying to find. He didn't blame the guy. This girl was gorgeous, and she moved with such grace and poise.

He followed from afar and saw her turn off the side road into a long driveway. He parked his car up the road and walked down the driveway until he saw her car parked outside a cottage.

He turned and walked back to his car and telephoned Peter. "I found her," he said.

Peter met him six hours later at his motel room. He led Peter to the driveway. Peter gave him the rest of his fee, and the detective left. Peter parked his car on the road, grabbed the roses, and walked down the driveway. He saw her car and almost started crying. He walked quietly up the porch stairs and knocked on the door.

Chapter 28

Elizabeth could hardly contain herself when Peter drove up to the front door of the condominium building. She hadn't seen her mother in months. She couldn't believe how excited she was and how happy she was to be back in the city.

"I didn't realize how much I missed my mother until now. I missed the city too. And of course, I missed you."

Elizabeth was rambling, and Peter was laughing.

"I don't need to tell you how much I missed seeing you every day and having you in my arms."

Elizabeth leaned over and kissed Peter quickly on the cheek and then ran out of the car and into the condominium building.

Peter had elected to drop Elizabeth off, letting them have the night to get caught up on each other's lives. Elizabeth had explained her need to get away from the dance world. She had felt like the walls were closing in on her. He was so glad that it was not something he had done. He had thought about their relationship hard and had not come up with a reason for her departure that would have involved the two of them. It was a relief to hear that it was her disenchantment with ballet. He was also glad to find out that she still had been dancing and planned to go back to dancing. He would not accept a gift like hers being wasted.

Monique waited nervously on the sofa. She had estimated how long it would take to drive from the cottage back to the city and home. She had missed Elizabeth so much and had so much to share with her.

Then she heard the key in the lock. Monique sprang up, and Elizabeth flew in. They met in the hallway.

"Mom," was all that Elizabeth could get out.

"My daughter," said Monique. "I missed you so much."

With tears rolling down her face, Elizabeth looked into her mother's eyes and said, "I'm so sorry for making you worry. Thank you so much for putting up with me."

There was laughing, crying, and lots of hugging and kissing. Never had two women demonstrated such joy in being reunited. It took five minutes for them to disengage and sit on the sofa.

Both women were talking at the same time, which prompted them to start laughing. They laughed out of nervousness. They laughed out of silliness, and they laughed out of love.

"You start," said Monique.

"Oh, Mom, you would not believe what happened."

"I'd like to find out what prompted you to want to stop dancing."

"I needed a break. I really did. I just felt like I had to get away. I would have left sooner or taken a vacation if I had thought of where to go. When I remembered the cottage, it was as if a lightning bolt struck me. I knew that was where

I had to go to sort things out. I don't know why. It was as if Gram was calling me home. It felt just like it did when I was younger. You know, we should never have stopped going there. The lake, the trees, the animals, the cottage . . . I can't explain how it all made me feel."

"I know, darling, but to leave and not contact me for a whole week."

"I know. I know. And I apologize for that. I'm really sorry. I thought you would try to convince me to come back and get help or something."

"Elizabeth, you should know by now that I would accept any decision you make. I would never try to undermine you. You must know that."

"Yes, yes. I realize that now. But then, I felt like I was choking, and I also felt like I was the one that had to fix myself. I didn't want any help. I didn't want any influence. I just wanted to be alone."

"It must have been scary out there all by yourself."

"No, actually, it wasn't," Elizabeth said.

She couldn't believe that she wasn't telling her mother about Michael Ryan. She had decided in the car not to tell anyone. She wanted to put the whole thing behind her and pretend that it had never happened. She wouldn't ever see him again anyway. And, really, he didn't mean anything to her or to anyone else. She felt guilty not telling her mother, but she reassured herself that it was much better that way. She wouldn't have to explain anything—the feelings, the longing, the sense of loss.

Monique prepared a light snack, and they even popped open a bottle of champagne. It went straight to Elizabeth's head, as she had not had a large amount of alcohol for months. Even Monique was lightheaded.

She was so lightheaded that she decided on the spur of the moment to tell Elizabeth about Jacques.

Elizabeth froze.

"What?"

"I think I've met a man. No, I'm sure that I've met a man. So sure, in fact, that I'm telling you about him."

"A man."

"A man."

"Mom, that's so great. I'm so happy for you. I've been hoping that some knight in shining armor would ride in and swoop you up."

"Well, he doesn't wear shining armor. He wears Armani, but I do believe he has managed to swoop me up."

Elizabeth couldn't believe it. She was so surprised and happy. She wondered why no one had ever come around courting Monique. *Another good thing that came from my leaving,* she thought.

"I can't wait to meet him. This is so exciting."

"He's heard all about you. I've been lucky that I've had Jacques to talk to while you were gone. He lives in Paris, and we manage to get away to see each other at least twice per month. He's trying to get me to go that next step, but I haven't had the courage or felt it was time to do so, yet."

"Yet."

Monique smiled. She knew she wanted to be with Jacques more than twice per month, but with Elizabeth away at the cottage and possibly needing her close to home, she had pushed Jacques away and avoided the question he so frequently asked.

"Wasn't it nice of Peter to give us this night alone," said Elizabeth.

"Peter is a pretty special man," Monique said quietly. "I can't believe that he hired a private detective to find you. He never told me a thing. He was so desperate to find you. He really does love you a lot, Elizabeth."

"I know, believe me, I know. He is special. He knocked on the door of the cottage at the perfect time. I needed someone to hold me. I felt alone, and there he was."

It had not occurred to Elizabeth that Peter just stepped in and filled the void that Michael Ryan had left in her life. The absence of Peter on a personal level had not left Elizabeth feeling something was missing in April. He was the first man in her life, and in April, she needed to be alone—without ballet and without a man. Now Peter had a purpose in her life; he was diminishing the loss of Michael.

"What a miracle," Monique added.

"We've made a decision, Mom. We're going to get married."

"Married?"

"Yes, as soon as we can make the arrangements. We're not going to live together. We're going to wait until our wedding night. I'm going to stay here with you, if that's okay."

"Of course, dear."

"We'll plan the wedding, and then I'll start thinking about auditioning for a ballet. I'd like to practice and practice and practice. I really have missed the dance studio and can't wait to get up on my pointers again."

"My goodness, you certainly aren't wasting any time."

"No, no. You can't waste time, Mom. I've come to realize that. Time waits for no one, as they say. And strange things happen in your life, even when you're not looking for anything to happen. I'd like to dictate what's going to happen in my life, a little bit more than I've been doing."

"Goodness. What went on at the cottage, anyway?"

"Nothing, Mother. Nothing. I just have come to some conclusions, and Peter is willing to take me back and commit to our life together."

"Good for him. I have always liked him, you know."

"I know."

"He adores you, and I know that he'll keep you safe."

After cleaning up after their light meal, Elizabeth went to her room. She showered and threw on her bathrobe. She felt at home in her room, but it didn't bring the peace that her loft bedroom did at the cottage. And Michael Ryan was not downstairs waiting for her to come out of her room. She wondered what he was doing and where he had gone. *I've got to stop thinking about him,* she thought. *That will not do me any good. He's probably lying down in a bed with another woman and having the time of this life.*

Chapter 29

September 2004

Mike had decided to ride to Connecticut. He figured that would be the farthest away from a biker gang he could go. He wanted to make sure that he wasn't in an area where there were a lot of gangs. He wanted to forget about the past and start anew. So he figured he would go where there were the fewest amount of motorcycles.

He had rented a room in a boarding house. It was like an upscale bed and breakfast establishment. The lady running the place was in her eighties, and he had convinced her to let him fix up a few things in lieu of rent.

Maggie James had always admired her ability to judge a human being. She looked at this young man with those brilliant blue eyes and agreed to his suggestion. She had given him an ultimatum, however. He had to cut that ridiculous ponytail off. She had no use for men with ponytails.

"There are quite a few things around here that need fixing up," Mike said to Maggie.

"Don't go thinking that I run a run-down dive here, young man."

"No, no, ma'am. That's not what I was saying. It's just that I'm real handy, and the break with the rent could help me out right now."

"Right now? You in trouble?" she asked.

"No, just trying to get myself back on track, and this seems as good a place as any. And I hear the landlady is quite a prize."

"Don't you go running at the mouth and trying to smooth me."

Maggie liked this young man.

"Now, I cannot tolerate that ponytail. It seems to me that a man should look like a man and not a teenaged girl."

Mike smiled. "Fine, I'll get a haircut. Do we have a deal?"

"Deal, yes. But I'm keeping my eye on you."

Much to Mike's surprise, he had no problems with Maggie's request. It was time, he thought, to change things.

It was quite a change when he looked at himself in the mirror. He had not cut his hair since his teens. The man looking at him from the mirror was a stranger. He would have to reacquaint himself with this person and make decisions about his life.

His first night at Maggie's place was spent tossing and turning. He dreamt of Elizabeth. She was dancing. She was swimming. She was preparing meals. She was doing lots of things, except talking to him. He so wanted to talk to her in his dreams, but she was moving around as if he didn't exist. He awoke in a sweat; he did not like the feelings he was having that night.

I wonder what she's doing, he thought. *She probably had her little dance, had a swim in the lake, and is fast asleep right now.*

Chapter 30

November 2004

Peter had held fast to New Year's Eve. He thought it would be exciting and romantic to get married on New Year's Eve, so Elizabeth went along with the idea. New Year's Eve in New York City it would be.

Elizabeth wanted to make sure that guest list wasn't too long. Neither she nor Peter had many family members— exactly one to be exact—Monique.

Peter had left his father's house when he was almost sixteen. He moved into a group home until he was eighteen and went to school on student welfare programs. His mother had died when Peter was fifteen. She fought terminal cancer for three years, but the disease finally took her. Just before her death, Peter revealed that he wanted to pursue ballet dancing. He had been enrolled in dance only because his mother loved dance. She had taken dance lessons in her youth and wanted Peter to experience some of the joys of dance that she had experienced.

Peter did more than experience the joys of dance. His abilities improved in leaps and bounds, and he was at the top of all his dance classes—especially ballet. He decided to focus on that genre. His father never did like any kind of dance. After his mother died, Peter was told that there would no longer be any dancing—especially ballet. Peter's father considered ballet to be "sissy." He refused to pay for further lessons and studio time. This was devastating to Peter at the time. Dance instructors began giving Peter free and reduced lessons. Peter got a part-time job to help pay for the lessons. Realizing his talents, girls would pay for the studio time so that Peter would partner up with them. This had taught him how to be a good male partner to the female ballerina.

When Peter's father found out about the continuation of the lessons, he gave Peter an ultimatum—"Quit dancing, and you can stay." Peter chose to leave. He never contacted his father again and had no intention of doing so. Peter's family was his dancing friends, instructors, and troupe members.

Like many top-ranked dancers, Elizabeth did not have many friends. She had been too busy to accumulate friends outside of the dance world. She, too, had friends and dancers as family.

Elizabeth did not want to invite any and every dancer in the city. She wanted to invite the closest friends to their wedding. She had been very fortunate and formed close relationships with female and male dancers from her early days as a young dancer. Those friends were part of lifelong relationships. Peter had a few friends from his early days as well. He would not have been able to exist without his dancer friends after leaving his father's home.

So the decision was made. The wedding would take place in a small chapel in Manhattan, and everyone would move into a penthouse suite at the Hilton downtown for the dinner and dance. The particulars would now have to be settled.

"I am exhausted, completely exhausted," Maria said.

"Me too," replied Elizabeth.

Maria and Elizabeth had been friends for almost twenty years. They had grown up together in the wonderful world of ballet. Maria was not a prima ballerina but a very good ballerina in her own right.

"I'm so excited about the wedding. Have you decided on your color scheme?"

"Oh God, it's these stupid little decisions that drive me crazy. Why can't you just wave a wand, and the perfect wedding just appears?"

"Honestly, Elizabeth, you're boring. Come on, this is supposed to be fun. How about pale pink? You said that you were going to wear a pair of ballet slippers—pale pink would be nice. Then I could wear a pale pink dress with white slippers. Peter could wear what he wants . . ."

Both girls started to laugh.

"He doesn't care, really. He just wants to make you his wife. Anyways, Peter and John could wear a pale pink rose on their lapels. What do you think?"

"I think you can go ahead and make all these silly plans. I feel like Peter. Let's just get this done."

"You're really not serious now. You have a great sense of style. And your mother. Your mother is the best."

"Yes, she's been nagging me about all these little details. Fine, then. It's pale pink and white. We'll get pink and white roses for the ceremony and the party. I'll get my mother to run with that color scheme and plan the tables and chairs and napkins and lights and whatever the heck she wants."

Maria rolled her eyes. Elizabeth would not be coerced into more planning. She wondered why Elizabeth wasn't more excited about this wedding.

"Your mother will be great for this, and I'm sure she'll take on this role with a big smile."

Elizabeth threw her towel at Maria, and both girls laughed and started talking about the upcoming production.

By the end of November, Elizabeth was in top dancing form, as was Peter. They had practiced together and had locked up a deal to dance in a production starting in March. They had discussed wedding plans and a December wedding seemed imminent. They would go on their honeymoon, return in the middle of January, and bust their buns to prepare for *Sleeping Beauty*.

Chapter 31

Mike had been a blessing for Maggie. She had gotten too old to do many things around the house. Mike needed a place to live, and she needed some help. It was a match made in heaven. He didn't go out much and kept to himself. There was something on his mind, and he was hiding it but not very well. Someone had hurt him. She wasn't sure if it was physical or emotional, but she knew that he was harboring some wounds.

Mike had cleaned out the entire garage in the back of the house. It had been a dumping spot for things over the years. He found only a few things that Maggie wanted to keep. She said that she really didn't need the space, so he asked her if he could set it up as a repair shop. She said, "Sure." So he started planning a shop. This time, it would be his place. He had found himself a job as a bartender at night and helped Maggie during the day. He also found time during the day to make shelves and start setting up his repair shop.

He didn't like nighttime. He was glad that he crawled home tired after bartending and got up early to help Maggie. She had four other boarders, and she provided meals for all of them. She also had two bed and breakfast rooms that were usually occupied. Everyone kept to himself or herself. They were together during meals, but no relevant or personal information was ever exchanged between the boarders. Mike liked to sit and talk with Maggie. They hit it off right away. She didn't pry into his past, for which he was grateful, and he didn't pry into her past. He had decided that she, also, had been hurt by someone in her past and that was why she busied herself running a bed and breakfast and boarding house. That way she could establish temporary relationships and didn't have to commit to anyone.

She knew that if she pushed, Mike would leave, and she was having way too much fun having him around. It had been a long time since she had developed a meaningful relationship with someone. This young man, in her opinion, was holding on to some deep kind of hurt. She did her best to let him know that she was there if he needed her.

Maggie couldn't help him at night, however. He tried not to think back to the time in the cottage, but he couldn't do it. He remembered how easy it was to fall asleep, to listen to the sounds of the lake and slowly drift off to sleep. At Maggie's place, his brain would not go to sleep. He couldn't stop thinking about Elizabeth. He wondered what she doing, and he knew he had let an opportunity slip through his fingers. It was an opportunity to tell her how he felt that he missed. He had made some really crappy decisions in his life, but he didn't have many regrets. He regretted not telling his mom how much she meant to him, and he regretted getting sucked into that bike gang. But everything else he did or tried, he had done so willingly and accepted the choices and the consequences. This was different. He felt he had chickened out, and he didn't have the guts to grab her, kiss her, and make love to her. He had never wanted a woman like that before. Women came and went, and he really didn't care. This woman, he cared about—a lot.

I've got to get her out of my mind, he thought. *I have to find another woman to keep my mind off of her.*

He had decided to start looking for a woman. He no longer wanted to go to bed alone at night. He no longer wanted to toss, turn, and think of someone he would probably never meet again. He wanted a woman in his life. *Yes, I have to find myself a woman.* With that thought and on this one night, Mike fell asleep.

He woke up the next day with a little more jump in his step. It seemed like he had turned a corner in his life.

"Well, aren't you full of piss and vinegar today," Maggie said as they ate breakfast together.

"Yup, you got that, Maggie, ole girl."

"What's got you so happy? Oh, it must be a woman."

"Well, you're almost right. It is a woman, but I haven't met her yet. I figured it's time for me to get back into the social world and check out the women in this town."

Maggie started to laugh. "Well, I thought maybe you were gay. I haven't seen you with a woman since you got here. It's a little strange for a young, good-looking guy like you not to have any women around."

"Well, that's gonna change, Maggie, my love. That's gonna change. I'll start checking out the scene at the bar tonight. So be prepared."

They both started laughing. It felt good to laugh. It had been a long time. When he thought about it, his life had not made him laugh very much.

Christmas was coming, and the bars in town were full at night. People were shopping during the day, and the Christmas celebrations continued at night. So Mike had no problem connecting with women, as there were tons of women hanging out at his bar. It was also not difficult for women to sit and talk with Mike. He was cute, with big blue eyes and dark brown hair, and he listened.

Two nights after he had made up his mind to find a woman, Mike struck up a great conversation with a woman named Mary. Mary was a realtor in town. She had been busy Christmas shopping for days and relaxed at night, sitting at the bar and talking with Mike. She stayed late that fourth night, until just about everyone had gone home. She had definitely given him some signals—positive ones. He got rid of the last customers, and before he locked up, he made his move.

"So, Mary, it looks like you might want to spend the night here."

"Well, maybe I do."

"Oh yeah? And where do you think you're gonna sleep, smarty?"

"Well, I don't see many places here to bunk out for the night. I was sorta hoping that some cute bartender guy would invite me over to his place."

Mike had hoped she would invite him over to her place, but he didn't think Maggie would object to him bringing Mary home. After all, she was pushing him to find a woman.

"It must be your lucky night. I just happen to know a bartender that wouldn't mind bringing you home with him."

They both laughed. Mike leaned over and wrapped his arm around Mary's waist, gave her a nice peck on the cheek, and led her out of the bar. They walked out with their arms around each other's waists and headed down the street. Mary had had a few drinks, so she didn't want to drive. Mike always walked to work. He lived just down the street from the bar. It was a beautiful December night. Snow had fallen earlier in the evening, and everything was white and glistening. Maggie's place was dark and quiet when they arrived, and they quietly went up to Mike's room.

"I'm pleasantly surprised," said Mary. "For a bartender, you keep a pretty neat room."

"You can thank my mother for that," said Mike.

It was a nice surprise for Mary. She had been watching him for weeks, and no women had appeared on the scene, so she had picked that night to snag him.

"Well, she taught you well. Where does a girl clean up around here?"

"Just down the hall to your right."

Mary went to the washroom down the hall to clean up a little and get ready. Mike was in his room pacing. He was nervous and didn't know why. The evening began nicely. Mike was a gentle and giving lover. Mary had fantasized about being with him, so she was ready to receive him. Mike had taken his time, even though it had been a long time since he had sex with anyone. He wanted to prolong the moment. They started off nice and slow, but they ended up fast and hard. Mary collapsed on the bed beside him. She had not been satisfied in a long time. She snuggled into his arm and laid her head on his chest. Mike put his arm around her.

Mary fell asleep in seconds, drifting into a wonderful sleep.

That was great, he thought. *That's exactly what I needed. Boy, I had a great time. Why the hell am I telling myself I had a great time? Why the hell am I not out cold like her? She's out cold, and so she should be. Why not me? Shit. Here I am again dying to fall asleep. Well, great idea, Mikey, ole boy. That was a great idea. Now what?*

By four Mike had fallen asleep. He couldn't understand why he had not gotten caught up in the emotion of the night. He came to the realization that Mary didn't mean anything to him. She just happened to be there. He was pissed off that he didn't feel fulfilled. He was pissed off that his last thoughts were about Elizabeth.

Chapter 32

Christmas was one week away, and that meant that her wedding day was two weeks away. Everything had been planned. Instead of a Christmas wedding, they had decided on a New Year's Eve wedding. Monique had helped her. It would be small but elegant. Their guests were mostly people from the ballet world and Monique's colleagues.

Jacques had come from France the week after Elizabeth returned home. She couldn't believe how her mother's face lit up when he was in the room. She could see the love they had for each other. She was sad that planning the wedding was slowing down their relationship. But she knew that nothing could really slow it down. They had been lucky to find each other later in life, and Elizabeth was so happy for her mother.

Monique and Elizabeth had visited France and stayed at Jacques's Paris apartment. It was absolutely beautiful. He had been the epitome of a great host. He showed them a side of Paris they had never seen before. Their visits to Paris had been all about fashion. Jacques showed them the French side of Paris—*la vie en Paris*.

"We're not going to spend our time at the haute couture houses," Jacques exclaimed.

Monique smiled. *"Non, mon cheri,* we'll follow your most wonderful lead."

"Oui, we will see Paris through a Parisian's eyes."

It was a wonderful time for both women. Elizabeth was ecstatic that her mother had found true love and in such a beautiful city.

"This afternoon, we shall spend it at the Rodin Museum. You can sit and stare at his most famous statue—*The Thinker*—and learn some great secrets about yourself while you sit and think with him."

Both women were amazed at the sights. Jacques was correct about *The Thinker.*

"What do you think he's thinking about, Mom?"

"I don't think that was the purpose of the sculptor," said Jacques. "It is said that he wanted people to think, not the man he sculpted. It is quite a contradictory theme for an artist, don't you think?"

"Interesting," said Elizabeth as she stared at the beautiful work of art.

In the evenings, they did what most Parisians do—went out for long dinners and great wine.

"I could get used to this," said Monique as she cuddled up to Jacques.

"Oui, ma cherie. That is the plan. Get used to this kind of life," Jacques said, laughing.

"This certainly is the most wonderful city. Everywhere you look, there is something beautiful and historic," interjected Elizabeth. "And the wine doesn't hurt."

All three laughed. They were becoming a family. Elizabeth loved to sit on the opposite side of the table and watch the love going back and forth between Jacques and her mother.

They toured Versailles and had lunch at the Eiffel Tower. Notre Dame Cathedral blew them away. Jacques was a font of information and history. It was obvious that he loved his city and he loved sharing the mystery and the wonder of Paris.

Everyone was exhausted at the end of the day, and Elizabeth retired to her bedroom, filled with the sights and sounds of Paris.

"It will be difficult to leave," said Monique.

"It is always difficult to leave Paris, *ma cherie*. I keep telling you that."

"Well, we have a wonderful event to attend in New York. My baby is getting married. I can't believe that she has grown up already."

"They grow up too fast on us," replied Jacques.

"Yes, they do."

Jacques grabbed his lady and gave a soft and passionate kiss.

"You do melt my heart," said Monique.

"That's the way it is supposed to be, *ma cherie*."

And with that, Monique and Jacques made wonderful love. They had found passion and joy in this later stage of life, and they weren't going to waste time.

"I love you," whispered Monique.

"Moi, non plus," replied Jacques.

With those words, they fell asleep with smiles.

He was going to spend Christmas Eve with his children in Paris and fly immediately to New York to spend Christmas Day with Monique, Elizabeth, and Peter. Everyone was excited.

Monique was floating through life. Her daughter was getting married to a wonderful young man. Elizabeth had returned home in good health and was rehearsing for another beautiful ballet. She had found love at fifty-eight. She couldn't believe it. He was a wonderful, kind, sexy, and passionate man. She had gone crazy shopping and couldn't wait to see the looks on everyone's faces when they opened their gifts. All the arrangements had been made for Elizabeth's wedding. They just needed to get their fittings for their dresses, and the rest of it should fall into place. This was a special time for her and her daughter. Their time had come, and she had worked hard for the moments in the coming week.

"Isn't this a wonderful time of year, Elizabeth?"

"The best, Mom. Now we have all these extra happenings to celebrate . . . weddings, great men, gifts, Paris, New York. It's great."

"Everything is set for your wedding, by the way. The florist is all set. Flowers are important, you know."

"Yes, Mother."

"Now, don't you minimize all these details. It's important. All the little points come together to create a most wonderful moment."

"I know. I'm sorry. I do appreciate everything you've done, really. It's just that there are so many little things that they start to overpower the main point—the marriage."

"Not this time. We will see the little details lead to the main event."

Both women smiled. It was getting exciting, and it was getting closer.

Chapter 33

Mary returned on December 27 from her holidays with her family. Mike and Mary had a quiet celebration at Mary's place.

She had a small bungalow in town, not far from her office and just down the street from Mike's bar. Nothing was really far from anything in Kramerville. Everyone knew everyone, and people looked out for each other. It was starting to develop, to the older residents' chagrin, but to the delight of the younger residents. Mary was busy in her realty business. They were not that far from New York City and the fancy Connecticut neighborhoods. Specialty boutiques and small-business people with young families were starting to move in. There was a lot of renovating going on and a lot of money changing hands. Mary had grown up in this town and was happy that she could continue to live there and make a good living.

Mary was delighted with her new day planner and impressed that Mike had it engraved. She would be using it a lot in the coming year. Mary gave Mike a new apron to wear at the bar. It said, "Who's the boss? I'm the boss." Mike had a small laugh over that gift. She also gave him a watch. She had noticed that he never wore a watch. He was quite pleased with this gift. He had never owned a watch and appreciated that she had noticed the absence of one.

They spoke of the coming year and talked about their goals. Mary had a goal of a certain number of sales per month. Mike's goal was to get that shop open and to repair Maggie's roof. It was a comfortable conversation. Neither person divulged any personal information, and neither person asked for any personal information. They liked it like that.

"You're pretty good on the computer," Mike said.

"I guess."

"I have an old friend that I've been looking for. We went to high school together in New York, and I've been wondering about him. Is there any way you can locate someone on the computer?"

"It's called the Internet." Mary sighed. "You really have to take a course or get someone to teach you how to get updated in this world. It's as if you've been out of touch with the real world for a while. You're not that old. You should be computer literate, a little bit."

"Nope, never used one. I never had reason to be on a computer."

"Well, you're missing out on lots. There are so many things you can look up, and you can plan things and you can check out things."

"What about people?"

"You could just type in someone's name and see what happens. There's also the White Pages phone book. You can actually access the phone books of any place in the world and look up a phone number. Most businesses now have websites—that would be an address on the computer. You can contact businesses on the computer and never use a telephone or letters again. It saves a lot of time and money. Time to get with it, Mr. Ryan."

Mike smiled. "I'll get there. Don't you worry about me."

Mike spent the night at Mary's place. He felt comfortable, and they had had a special celebration. He woke up before Mary and went home to shower and change. He had a great night with Mary, but he was more excited about the information she gave him. After breakfast, he told Maggie that he was going to town to check on a few things and that he would return and shovel her drive and sidewalk for her.

He was saving Maggie a lot of work. At her age, shoveling snow was one of the things she hated the most. She wondered what he was checking out in town. He had a faraway look in his eyes during breakfast. She was starting to depend on Mike more and more each day. She knew that he meant more to her than just a boarder. He felt more like a son now—the son she had lost so many years ago.

"What are you up to?" she asked.

"Nothing. What makes you think I'm up to something?"

"Woman's intuition. I know you're up to something."

"Who? Me? Never. Don't you worry, Maggie, ole girl. I'll be back to shovel that snow."

"I'm not worried about the snow. I'm worried about you. Anything you'd care to talk about?"

"Nope. When did you start being so nosey? Everything's fine. I'm going down the street and into town for a while. What's the big deal?"

"No big deal. Just noticing."

"Notice making dinner. I'll be needing some feeding when I'm finished shoveling. See you in a bit."

"See you in a bit."

Chapter 34

Mike could not remember the last time he walked into a library. His mother had taken him to one once, and they had sat on the floor in the kiddy section and read books together. He remembered as he entered and inhaled the smell of books, lots of books. She had read to him and wrapped her arms around him all afternoon. Calm and security filled Mike's heart and soul. It was a special time for them.

Maybe she's telling me that I'm doing the right thing.

He walked up to the desk where a friendly-looking lady in her fifties welcomed him.

"Hello, I haven't seen you in here before, have I?"

"No, no. This is my first visit to this library."

"Well, what can I do for you?"

"I've heard that there are computers available in the library for people to use."

"Yes, yes, that's true. They're over on the back wall. We only have four of them, but we are expecting to increase our inventory in the coming year."

"Great. Do you pay if you use them? Or does it cost anything to borrow them?"

"No. But you should have a library card, just in case you want to print something or the Internet refers to a book in the library to borrow."

"Okay, then. I guess I'll get myself a library card."

"It will cost two dollars," she said. "Now if you could fill out all your information on this sheet, we'll get the card for you."

Mike filled out the information. He felt like a little kid getting his first bankbook. He remembered getting a bankbook too. So many memories were flooding into his mind these days.

"So, you're living at Maggie's. You must be that nice young man that's helping Maggie fix up her place. She's real happy that you're there to help her out. When we get together to do some quilting, she talks a lot about you. It's nice to meet you, Mr. Ryan."

"Mike, please."

"Mike, it is. Now, here's your new card. It will cost you a dollar to replace it, so put it in a safe place. The computers, as I said, are along the back wall." She pointed toward the back of the library.

"Thanks."

Mike walked over to the back wall, and there they were, four computers, just like she said. *Shit,* he thought. *I don't even know how to turn the stupid thing on. What the hell was I thinking? I can't get Mary to help me look up a woman, for God's sake. Why would you look up a woman from high school and why would you get your current woman to help you? I don't think that would go over too well. But how in the hell am I gonna figure out how to use this thing?*

He sat down in front of one of the monitors and stared at it. He looked and looked for an on/off switch. He checked both sides and couldn't find a thing. He hadn't noticed that a very precocious nine-year-old girl had sat beside him.

"Whatcha doin'?" she asked as she tapped him on the arm.

Mike jumped. "Nothing, I've never used this model of machine before, and I'm having trouble turning it on."

"It's over here, silly," she said as she moved his hand to the silver button.

The machine clicked on and starting making noises as it was booting up. Her computer had been turned on as well.

"My name is Rebecca," she said.

"Oh, my name is Mike. But you shouldn't talk to strangers."

"Oh, you're not a stranger. Miss Campbell told me that a new guy in town was on the computers and that I wasn't supposed to bother you. Am I bothering you?"

"No, no, that's fine. Thanks for showing me how to turn on the computer."

"Okay."

Rebecca started punching keys on the keyboard, and various sights and sounds came from her computer. She was bringing up images of zoo animals doing silly things and laughing. Mike couldn't believe what was coming out of that monitor. *A whole new world*, he thought. This little girl was creating a whole new world in tiny Kramerville.

She could visit anywhere. *So now how do I get to look up things on this freaking thing?*

"Is there something wrong?" Rebecca asked. Mike had been looking over her shoulder for about twenty minutes.

"Well, you look like you're pretty good on this thing."

"My mom gets mad because she says I'm on the computer too much. I really like it. I follow the rules and don't look at things I'm not supposed to. The library has blocked all those bad places anyway. But if Miss Campbell catches you on a bad site, she'll call your parents and then suspend you from using the computers. So I follow her rules."

"Yeah, you have to follow the rules. Hey, would you know how to look things up on this thing?"

"What do you mean? Is it a bad thing?"

"No, no, not a bad thing. I'm trying to find an old friend, and I can't figure out how to do it."

"You don't use computers much, do you?"

"No, I don't, Rebecca. But I was hoping that maybe you could teach me. Would that be okay? I'd appreciate the help, and then I can learn to do it myself. You never know. I could get as good as you."

Rebecca giggled. She liked this man. He was silly. Didn't everyone know how to use the Internet?

"Do you know where this person lives?" she asked.

"Yup, New York."

"What's his name?"

"Her name. Her name is Elizabeth Hamilton."

"Elizabeth Hamilton. Hmm, there's a ballet dancer named Elizabeth Hamilton. I know that because I take ballet lessons. Do you like ballet?"

"Yes, yes, I like it a lot."

"Really? I love ballet, almost as much as the computer. I'm not taking lessons right now because we're having a Christmas vacation, but I start again next week. I like the music and the clothes and everything. My mother used to dance when she was a little girl."

Oh, oh, this kid is gonna talk and talk.

"Okay, so how do we check up on Elizabeth Hamilton on the computer?"

"And," she added, "there's a big picture of her dancing in my dance studio. Maybe it's your friend?"

"Well, let's find out. How about showing me how to find this woman."

"Okay, first you type in her name. I'm sure that we'll get lots of hits on her name. Or we could just type ballet."

"How about her name?"

"Okay, we'll start with her name."

Up popped a lot of search results.

"See, lots of sites mention Elizabeth Hamilton. You see, she's pretty famous. Which one do you want to see first?"

"How do you look at these things?"

"You move this little arrow, see, using this thing—it's called a mouse." You click with your finger like this twice, and then it opens that site or address. See, it's not hard."

So, they clicked one of the websites, and up popped Elizabeth's face. Mike inhaled quickly. He couldn't believe it. It had taken all of three seconds to come up with a picture of her. *Wow.*

"That's amazing," he said.

"She's pretty, isn't she? Okay, let's see what they say about her. You wanna see that?"

"Yes, okay, let's look at that."

There was a summary of Elizabeth's ballet history in Wikipedia. There were photos of her dancing and a long list of accolades of various ballet critics. He knew she was special by the way she moved on the deck at the cottage. He couldn't keep his eyes off of her. He sat in total amazement. *How could someone like her take off all that time to take care of someone like me, someone she didn't even know?*

"Is there any way we can get her address or something?"

"I doubt it," said Rebecca. "Rich people don't give out their addresses. They're what you call—unlisted."

"Yeah, well can we find out anything that could sorta tell us where she is?"

"Maybe she's dancing somewhere. Maybe we can look up ballets."

"Okay, go, kid."

"Kid. I'm not a kid. I'm nine years old, and I'm going to be ten in April. So, I'm pretty grown up."

"Sorry, sorry. How's buddy? Can I call you buddy?"

"Buddy's okay. I'll ask my mom if we can be buddies. I'll check with Miss Campbell too."

So back to the Ballets, Mike thought.

"Okay, here's a list of ballets going on. You wanna check New York?"

"That might be a good idea."

"I don't see her name anywhere. She danced in one last year, look. But she didn't finish it; she left, and someone else danced in her place. I remember that story because Mademoiselle was gonna go and see her and she cancelled her tickets when she heard that it wasn't being danced by Miss Hamilton."

"Nothing, eh?"

"Well, we can check other places. That's what's nice. You can always find other places to get your stuff, if you take the time."

"Okay, buddy."

"Not yet, remember? I have to get permission. So, for now, you have to say Rebecca."

"Okay, Rebecca, you're the boss."

What's with kids these days?

"Look, I found something. She's going to be dancing a new ballet starting in the spring. She will be the lead dancer with her partner Peter Rogers. Hey, that's the partner she was with before. Hey, I remember now. They're getting married."

"What?"

Mike's heart dropped. "Married." *Oh no,* he thought, *I'm too late.* "Are you sure about that?" He swallowed hard. He couldn't believe it. Yes, he could. Why would a woman of her beauty and kindness not be with someone? What kind of an idiot was he anyway? Did he really think that she would be on her own? Did he really think that she was sitting around thinking about him as he was thinking about her?

Mike thanked Rebecca for her help and said that he hoped he would see her again soon in the library.

Rebecca said that she would be asking permission to see if they could be buddies.

Mike walked very slowly back to Maggie's place. *She's getting married.* That's all he could think of. *You should've left well enough alone,* he thought. *Now, you're just gonna keep thinking about this marriage of hers.*

Chapter 35

Monique looked at Elizabeth. She couldn't believe how beautiful she looked. It was two days before New Year's Eve, and they were both getting fitted for the final time. Elizabeth stood on the stand for the seamstress to check the hem. Everything was perfect. Monique's fitting had already finished. Now she sat and watched her beautiful daughter get ready for her special day.

"Are the butterflies flying around in your tummy yet, honey?" she asked her daughter.

"A few flutters now and then, Mom."

"Oh, honey, I'm getting so excited. Everything is ready, and I think New Year's Eve is a perfect night for a wedding. We'll start 2005 properly, and you and Peter will go off to Cuba for your honeymoon. It just sounds so great, doesn't it?"

"Yes, yes, it does."

What was that in her voice? Yes, it does—of course, it does. Something's missing here. Where's the sparkle? I haven't seen the sparkle since last June. Putting this dress on should have produced the sparkle.

"Everything okay, Elizabeth?"

"Pardon, yes, of course everything's okay. Why do you ask?"

"I don't know—mother's intuition, I guess. It just seems that something is bothering you. Is there something bothering you?"

"Me? No, Mom, nothing's bothering me. I'm getting married to a great guy. My mom seems to be in love with a very sexy Frenchman, and my new ballet will be opening soon. What could possibly make you think there's something wrong?"

"You know, Gram is with us."

"I know. I miss her too. I really wish she was here in person. But I know that she's looking and smiling and wondering why the heck you're questioning me like this."

They both started laughing. Moreover, they were both wishing Constance was with them in body, not just in spirit.

Monique stopped questioning Elizabeth, much to her joy. She was glad that her mother thought that maybe her sorrow of not having Gram around was causing this hesitation about the wedding. She did wish her grandmother was there, but it was something else. She really wasn't sure what was bothering her, but she did know that something was gnawing at her thoughts. She hadn't been sleeping well, and even in rehearsal she found that she was losing her concentration.

It's just nerves about the wedding. Every bride goes through the same thing. I just have to wait until all this hullabaloo is over with. I can go to Cuba and relax and come back and bust ass.

After the wedding dresses were taken care of, the women tried on their dresses for the rehearsal party that evening. They had decided to wear the same color. Monique had been against it, but Elizabeth thought it was a great idea. They decided to go with red. There was a difference between the outfits. Monique detailed her outfit with black, and she had black accessories to set off the red. Elizabeth detailed her outfit with white, and she wore pearl accessories. Both were delighted with their outfits. They had chosen them during a shopping trip to Paris. They knew that they were outfits that were different from anything that was available in New York.

Peter was going to wear a black suit, white shirt, and white tie. Jacques was going to wear a black suit, a white shirt, and a red tie. It was going to be a very well-put-together wedding party.

There were going to be only two attendants for the ceremony, Maria as the maid of honor, and John as the best man. Both Elizabeth and Peter had wanted to avoid making choices from their friends. Maria and John were their oldest friends, and everyone knew that. They did not want to insult anyone, so they chose only two. It made it seem a little more personal and familial anyway.

The rehearsal party was being held in a small ballroom at the Trump Towers. They had gone to the chapel for their quick rehearsal and then hopped into a limousine for the party. Only a few close friends were in attendance for the party.

Someone from the society pages had asked to take pictures at the chapel. Elizabeth eventually said yes after Monique begged her to do so. She was in the magazine business, she said, and it didn't look good if she didn't support the press.

So the next day in the society pages of the *New York Times*, there were colored pictures of the wedding party at the rehearsal. It was a great picture. Elizabeth even said that she would like to contact the photographer to get a good copy of the picture for their album. She thanked Monique for convincing her to allow the story. "It would also be great publicity for your new ballet," Monique had said.

December 30, 2004. I'll be married in two days, Elizabeth thought. She had just finished her last rehearsal for two and half weeks, and she was thinking while she was stretching. *Why am I not over the moon right now? What is it with me lately?*

She jumped when someone tapped her on the shoulder.

"Sorry," said Peter. "I thought you saw me coming in the mirror."

"No, I had my eyes shut, and I was concentrating on stretching. Quite the surprise—a nice one."

Peter lifted her chin and gave her a wonderfully soft kiss. "I can't wait until we're married. I'm looking so forward to getting away and just being alone. Aren't you?"

"Yes, it sounds so wonderful to lie around on a beach and do nothing. The pictures of the resort look so beautiful. It seems like a wonderland."

"Well, princess, it will be our wonderland. Time is not going fast enough. Tomorrow night is not coming fast enough in my opinion."

Time, I wish I had more time. Why? I should be thrilled about tomorrow night. What's holding me back? I just don't understand it.

"The guys are taking me out tonight. We're going to go out for dinner and then to the traditional strip club. I promise I won't look."

They both laughed. The idea of Peter at a strip club amused both of them.

"I'd love to be there," she said. I would pay to see the look on your face when they pay someone to give you a lap dance. No touching, mister."

"Babe, you don't have to worry about me. Just the thought of one of those women on my lap gives me chills."

"Yeah, that's until she's shaking all her things at you."

Again, they laughed. Peter sat and stretched awhile with Elizabeth. They loved rehearsing and dancing and all the hard work associated with it. Similar worlds connect easily. There were many similarities between them, and Peter thought that was the reason their union would last forever.

Monique and Elizabeth had planned to have dinner together. They had reservations at their favorite French restaurant. They were going to get all dressed up for their last meal before Elizabeth became Peter's wife. Elizabeth was looking forward to the quiet time with her mother.

Monique was almost finished getting dressed for dinner. She looked at her reflection in the mirror and liked what she saw. *"I don't look too bad for an old broad,* she thought. *I hope I can make a great mother of the bride tomorrow night. I can't wait to see Elizabeth in that chapel.*

The knock on the door brought Monique back to reality.

"Just about ready, Mom?"

"Yes, honey, come on in. I'm almost done. I just have to get these earrings on."

"Hey, you look great."

"Why, thank you, and you look wonderful yourself. Is that a new outfit?"

"Yes, it is. I thought this special night deserved a special dress. The next time I wear it, it will remind me of being with you."

Their eyes met with a knowing love. They had been so close for twenty-four years. Monique had cherished Elizabeth's existence from the moment she was born. There was never any regret in her decision to keep her child. She knew that she would love and protect that little person her whole life. And now she was getting married and ready to move away from her. It was a bittersweet evening for Monique.

The restaurant was full of hustle and bustle. It was the holidays, and people looked like they were celebrating the New Year early. People were smiling at every table. People looked up as the two women moved toward their table. Elizabeth's dressed flowed as she moved. She had left her long blonde hair down and loose. It, too, flowed as she walked. Monique walked behind her and smiled because she could see the looks that Elizabeth was creating as she moved. *That's my beautiful baby,"* she thought.

They decided to splurge and order a bottle of expensive champagne. They also ordered decadent desserts after dinner. While finishing up her dessert, Monique looked at her daughter. Elizabeth seemed a hundred miles away. She was playing with the chocolate mousse, not really eating it. She twirled her spoon around and around. *What is that look? There it is again,* thought Monique.

"Penny for your thoughts."

"What? Oh. Sorry, Mom. I guess I was daydreaming. I don't think I can put another spoonful of anything into my body. I'm going to pop the buttons on this dress."

"I don't think you have any worry about popping any buttons, honey. That's the least of our worries. However, what were you thinking about? You seemed to be hundreds of miles away."

"Nothing, really. I was just thinking about the fact that this would be our last meal together as me being a daughter. I've been a granddaughter and a daughter my whole life. I wish I was still a granddaughter, but that won't be anymore. I'll still be a daughter, I know. But after tomorrow night, I'm going to be a wife . . . a wife. That's an important role for me."

"Of course, it is. Are you having any doubts?"

"No, no. I don't think so. I've just had this feeling since just before Christmas that something wasn't right. I'm not sure what it is. Maybe I'm just scared of the unknown.

Maybe I'm a little hesitant about changing my life. I'm enjoying it so much now."

"Have you talked to Peter about this?"

"No. It doesn't have anything to do with Peter. It's just something inside of me. Let's not get too caught up about it, shall we. Let's just enjoy the evening."

"Okay, let's."

Nevertheless, Monique was worried. There had been no sparkle in those green eyes of hers. She had been looking for it since Christmas. *Why the hell isn't there a sparkle? A bride-to-be should be sparkling. Am I looking for a problem where there isn't one?*

Chapter 36

Mike was staring at the computer monitor. Sam, the guy in the room beside him, had a computer in his room. Sam had left his room door open, and Mike had passed by and seen the monitor on the little desk.

When Sam came back upstairs, Mike asked if Sam could look something up on the computer for him. Sam said, "No problem."

"Well, that's one beautiful woman. Do you know this girl?"

"She's an old friend. I heard she was getting married and thought I'd be able to get in touch with her to get some of the details."

"Well, let's see if there are any recent stories about her."

"You can do that?"

"Yeah, sure no problem. We have her name and what she does."

The article about her rehearsal at St. Raphael's Chapel popped up on the monitor. *There she is,* he thought. *And there's the groom. Shit. A groom.*

"Looks like she's getting married in this church tonight," Sam told Mike.

"What?"

"Yeah, it's gonna be a New Year's Eve wedding—an early ceremony and a great big New Year's Eve party. Oh the rich know how to do it, don't they?"

"Yeah, they certainly do. Can you get the address of that church, Sam?"

"Yeah, that's an easy one. What, you gonna go up to New York and surprise this girl?"

"Uh, I don't know. I'm gonna think about it. I've got plans for tonight, but I could look her up later on."

"Well, here it is . . . 753 Bond Street, Manhattan. Nice area. Of course, I didn't figure it would be in Harlem."

Sam started to laugh and wrote down the address down for Mike. He printed up a copy of the map so that Mike could see exactly where the church was. Mike thanked Sam and went in the room.

He sat on his bed staring at the piece of paper. *She's getting married. Well, I guess now I can put the whole thing behind me—bikes, cottages, and ballerinas. That's it, Mikey, just put it behind you and get on with it.*

Mike called Mary to confirm their meeting at the bar. Mike had to work, unfortunately, but they would be together for midnight and could share a New Year's kiss. Mary didn't seem upset about the whole thing, and that was cool with Mike. He didn't need a clingy woman; he just needed some company.

I need to get my shit together before I start making plans with any woman. Stop thinking about women, stupid. Just go to work. Just go to work.

Chapter 37

The wedding ceremony was to start at 5:00 p.m. They had begged the preacher to allow them to get married on New Year's Eve. They had agreed to an early ceremony; they would have agreed to a noon ceremony. They weren't very religious, but they wanted a small chapel with a nondenominational ceremony and a nice party afterward. They had planned to stay until midnight and leave shortly after. They had booked the honeymoon suite in the same hotel, and they were to fly to Cuba the next afternoon.

Elizabeth had packed for the honeymoon, and her bags were ready to go. She had packed a separate bag for her wedding night. She was now getting together a few things she thought she would need during the wedding. They would take a limo to the church, and then the limo was to bring them to the hotel for the party and dinner. They had booked the room for the whole evening.

Monique had done a wonderful job choosing and editing all the little details of the chapel and party ambiance. They had decided that it would all be a surprise for Elizabeth and Peter. Agreeing to have professional magazine photographers was a big leap for Elizabeth, but Monique wouldn't have taken no for an answer. Before dinner, the photographers would take pictures of their guests and the wedding party. Eight o'clock was to be the start of dinner, after the cocktail Hour. Signature pink drinks had been added to the bar menu. With a multitude of candles, Monique created a most ethereal and magical backdrop for her daughter's special day.

Elizabeth would have all her bags brought to the honeymoon suite when they arrived at the hotel. Organization and planning were important to her. Keeping stress at a minimum was important. The little uncertainty nagging in the back of her mind would lie low if she kept her stress level down. So everything was set. Why did she think something was missing, something was wrong?

I have to get this silliness out of my mind. What the heck is wrong with me? This is supposed to be the happiest day of my life. I have to get myself together and get this job done.

"How's the bride doing?" Monique asked from outside Elizabeth's door.

They had returned from the hair salon. They had their makeup done, and both of them looked great. All that was left was to get dressed and hop into the limo. The photographer was going to arrive soon. Monique had wanted to get some before chapel pictures. One of the best photographers at the magazine was going to take all the pictures, and Monique was excited. She knew how beautiful they were going to turn out. He was doing her a huge favor and would not take any money. She would have to get him one huge gift for this.

"Fine."

"Can I come in?"

"Yes, yes, of course, Mom. How are you doing?"

As she opened the door, Monique said, "I'm fine, honey. I'm starting to get really excited. John Franks will be here soon to take some pictures. We'd better start getting dressed. I think I should get myself finished first, and then we'll save the wedding dress until the last minute. What do you think?"

"That's sounds like a good plan, Mom. Don't start getting mushy and excited. Streaking makeup is not flattering. We're going to keep level heads, at least until we get into that limo."

They both laughed, and Monique left to get dressed. *No sparkle, no sparkle.*

Monique was ready and now headed to Elizabeth's room. Jacques had put all their bags by the front door. Jacques and Monique were staying at the same hotel that night. They had wanted to be able to celebrate and crash all in the same place. They figured they would stay behind until the last guest left, and then they'd celebrate the New Year in private. She was anticipating a great 2005.

Monique gasped when she entered Elizabeth's room. Her dress was hanging on the closet door, and when Elizabeth turned to greet her, Monique couldn't believe how beautiful Elizabeth was. She had grown into the most confident and beautiful woman. Tears were beginning to form in her eyes. She had to breathe slowly and deeply so that she didn't start crying.

"Okay, sweetie, all ready to get into that thing?"

"As ready as I'll ever be."

It took about five minutes for them to avoid the hair, avoid the makeup, and try to avoid wrinkling the wedding dress. It was a simple dress that draped Elizabeth's body perfectly. The bottom half of the dress flared out and flowed when she walked. Her new ballet slippers shimmered underneath. They had been made with the most beautiful pale pink silk, and the pink satin ribbons were crossed expertly up her ankles. She was a vision.

The doorbell rang, and in walked John Franks and his assistants to take the pictures. Both women inhaled and smiled at each other.

"Let the games begin," Monique said.

Chapter 38

They were sitting in the limousine on the way to the church. Elizabeth was by herself on one seat, with her bouquet of white roses on the seat beside her. Jacques and Monique were facing her. John Franks had gone ahead to get ready for the chapel pictures. Monique knew she didn't have to worry about the picture aspect of the day. It was such a relief. Now she just had to worry about her daughter. Moreover, she didn't know why she had that feeling—that little anxious feeling casting doubts in her mind about her daughter's elation—or lack of it.

"Everything okay, honey? Monique asked Elizabeth.

"Yes, Mom. Everything is fine. What's got you worried? Everything is ready. Everything is planned, and now all we have to do is do it."

"Elizabeth is right, *ma cherie*," said Jacques. "Just relax and enjoy this wonderful evening we have planned. All will be *magnifique*."

"I'm sure you're both right. However, as the mother of the bride, it's my right to worry that everything will go off as planned. It's my last right as a mother."

"Oh, now there's a statement."

"Well, you know what I mean. I know that I'll always be your mother."

"You can say that again."

"But we're moving into a different phase."

"Now, Mom, I told you not to get mushy until we get to the church. We don't want to arrive with soap opera mascara running down our faces now, do we?"

"No, no, dear. No tears. No mascara."

"Remember, you're going to be gaining a son after tonight."

"Yes, a son."

"There will be three of us again."

"Three of us."

"And maybe we can make that four soon."

"What? Now, Elizabeth, let's just concentrate on your wedding, shall we?"

Jacques squeezed her hand. Nothing would make him happier than making this woman his wife and making this girl his daughter. He was looking forward to getting the wedding between Elizabeth and Peter finished so that he could ask Monique to share her life with him. *But one thing first,* he thought.

"*Oui*, it will be a beautiful evening," Jacques added.

"The crowds are beginning to gather for the dropping of the New Year's Eve ball," said Elizabeth. "We're lucky to get ahead of the chaos. New Year's Eve is always special in New York City."

"Always," said Monique. "We're going to stay put in the hotel so we don't have to worry about the madness and the crowds."

"It will be beautiful and perfect," said Jacques. "My two beautiful women now have to sit back and enjoy the evening. Maybe we should have opened a bottle of champagne before we left, just to get everyone relaxed?"

Everyone laughed.

"I don't know about that," said Monique. "We'd probably be giggling and falling asleep. We don't want to do either of those things right now. Decorum is the order of the day."

"*Oui, ma cherie.* I suppose you are right. But we would be having *un moment superbe.*"

They arrived at the hotel with time to spare. Rushing was not needed.

I'm ready, she said to herself as she alighted from the limousine.

Peter was already in the church. He was in the groom's waiting room. Jacques came into the room, and his heart started beating faster. This meant that Elizabeth was here, and in a few minutes, they would be married. He was so happy and could not believe his luck in finding this most special woman. She shared his heart's love and his dancing love. They would share a wonderful, long marriage, and he couldn't wait.

Guests slowly started filling up the chapel. It was not a huge guest list. It was perfect for the chapel. St. Raphael's Chapel seated approximately sixty people comfortably. Tonight, there would be forty guests, two attendants, a bride, a groom, and a preacher. There were about four people involved with photography. They would also be joining everyone for dinner. Once dinner started, Elizabeth didn't want any more pictures taken. She wanted everyone to sit and enjoy the rest of the evening.

Peter came out of the groom's waiting room with Jacques and positioned himself to the left of the preacher. A harpist played beautiful music to set the scene.

Beethoven's *Moonlight Sonata* began. It was Elizabeth's favorite piece of music. She had wanted to walk down the aisle to this piece of music. Everyone turned to face the back of the chapel. Monique and Elizabeth came up the aisle, hand in hand.

This is it, she thought. *This is the last few minutes of being a single woman. Peter looks so great. He has tears in his eyes. I am one lucky woman.*

Monique squeezed Elizabeth's hand, and both women looked at each other and smiled. *There still isn't any sparkle. Oh God, where's the sparkle? There should definitely be a sparkle now. Nothing can beat this moment.*

Monique was dreading handing her daughter over to Peter. She knew that this was another chapter of a daughter's life, but she didn't have to like it. Down the aisle, the two women continued. Guests were smiling and whispering about Elizabeth's beauty and grace. Maria was standing to the left of the justice of the peace. John was on Peter's left, to the right of the justice. Time seemed to go slowly, although it took only a minute to reach the altar. Elizabeth kissed Monique on the cheek and handed her over to Peter.

Peter leaned over and kissed Monique, as well. It was a nice touch. Monique took her place to the right of Jacques. They were ready to begin.

They had chosen to have the traditional marriage vows. They decided to have their personal statements said at the wedding reception. Everything was going perfectly. Monique had dabbed at her eyes a few times, but there was no soap opera mascara. They would soon be husband and wife.

"If anyone here has any reason why this man and this woman should not be joined together in holy matrimony, let them speak now or forever hold their peace," announced the preacher.

There was a slight, silent pause.

"Stop." The doors of the chapel had been thrown open, and there was a man at the back of the church.

Everyone turned at the same time.

The man started coming forward. "Stop the wedding," he said. "I have an objection." As the man came forward, Elizabeth started to recognize him. It was Michael Ryan. She could not believe her eyes.

What's happening? she thought.

"Who the hell is this guy?" yelled Peter.

"Peter, I know this man. Let me see what the matter is."

"What? You know him? What the hell is he doing? What does he mean he objects? Who is this guy?"

Elizabeth handed her bouquet to her mother, and their eyes met.

Oh God, there's the sparkle, thought Monique.

Elizabeth started walking toward Michael Ryan. He could not believe what he was doing. He had driven his motorcycle from Connecticut into New York, nonstop. Every speed limit and red light had been ignored. The fact that he didn't get stopped by the police was a miracle. Police loved to stop motorcyclists.

He had decided to let his feelings be known. *At least,* he thought, *she'll know.* He didn't realize that a motorcycle ride to New York was not as easy in the dead of winter as on a nice summer day.

Both Mike and Elizabeth's arms were outstretched forward, and just as they touched, the shot rang out through the church.

Mike's eyes widened as he looked at Elizabeth. She tried to grab him, but he fell forward onto the floor.

Mayhem broke out in the church. People started screaming. People started hiding in the pews. Jacques grabbed Monique and pulled her behind the altar. Peter ducked down, but his feet were frozen where they stood. There was no protection, but he just knelt and kept staring at Elizabeth.

The only sound people heard was the sound of the front doors opening and closing and the then the sound of Michael Ryan's labored breathing.

"Someone call 911!" Elizabeth screamed as she turned Michael over to look at him. He was bleeding heavily from his back. Her hands were shaking.

Oh God, she thought, *not again.*

Their eyes met when she turned him. He was lying on her wedding dress, bleeding everywhere. She crumpled pieces of her dress and pressed it against the wound to try to stop the bleeding.

"Did I make in time?" he asked.

"Yes," replied Elizabeth.

"I had to come to at least tell you what I didn't say before."

"Elizabeth!" exclaimed Peter. "What the hell is going on?"

"Peter, this is a friend of mine."

"Friend? Friend? Are you crazy? He's been shot. Who the hell has a wedding and a shooting at the same time? I don't understand."

"I know, I know. Please just help me stop the bleeding; otherwise he's going to die. Do you want him to die?"

"No, no. Of course, I don't want him to die," he yelled.

Monique ran from the altar with Jacques close at her heels.

"Elizabeth, Elizabeth," she yelled. "Oh my God, are you hurt?"

"No, Mom, no I'm fine. This is Michael Ryan. He's hurt."

"Michael Ryan? Who's Michael Ryan?"

"The man from the cottage."

"The cottage. Oh, the cottage."

"The cottage?" asked Peter. "What does that mean?"

"Nothing, dear," said Monique. "Let's not think about that right now. Now we have to get this man to a hospital."

Michael Ryan's eyes remained closed. Elizabeth would not let go of his hand. The paramedics arrived, and they quickly got him into the ambulance, as it was obvious that he was bleeding out. Elizabeth got into the ambulance with him, turned to her mother and Peter, and said, "Please meet me at the hospital." The doors closed, and the ambulance sped off.

Inside the ambulance, the paramedics were hooking Michael up to IV tubes and tried to increase the pressure on his wound to slow down the blood loss. They weren't far from the hospital, so they thought that this guy might have a chance to make it.

Just before they reached the hospital, Michael Ryan opened his eyes. He looked at Elizabeth. She was so beautiful, he thought. "Please don't leave me. I love you," he said. His eyes closed again, and the heart monitor registered a straight line.

Chapter 39

November 2004

Big Al could not get Mikey out of his mind. No one lived after screwing him. He had to get the last word. He had to find Mikey and kill him; that's all there was to it.

Big Al went back to the approximate place where the beating took place. He went to the closest town. He figured that Mikey had to have visited a close place, because he was too hurt. *How did he survive? How did he heal? There had to be a doctor close by.*

No one in town had seen an injured man or an injured biker. Big Al had gotten a private detective to ask the questions, because no one really wanted to talk to him. They were scared of him. The private eye did find out that a woman had bought a whole lot of first-aid supplies around the time of the beating. No one really knew if anyone lived with her, but she had been around for the whole summer. She was a beautiful girl who just came in every now and then and bought some groceries and some supplies. Everyone did remember the beautiful blonde that seemed to float when she walked. "A nice, quiet young lady. A beautiful girl who always had a smile on her face."

Finally, the private eye got a name—not the girl's name, but the name of the person who owned the cottage—Constance Hamilton. When they investigated the name Constance Hamilton, they found out that she had died. They went to the cottage and didn't find anything special. There was nothing around to indicate that anyone was living there at that time. It looked like the place had been closed. There were some tools in the garage, but there were no vehicles.

The private detective got lucky when he punched "Hamilton" in the computer. A few people popped up, and then a beautiful blonde's face popped up. She was a ballerina from New York City. The private eye took the pictures to the little town to see if anyone recognized the picture of Elizabeth Hamilton.

"Hey, that's her—the lovely girl that was staying at the Hamilton cottage. I know that Connie had a granddaughter; that must be her."

Now, they had a name, a cottage, and a city. Big Al could not figure out the connection between Mikey and this ballerina chick, but he could feel something. He knew he was on the right track.

At the end November, the detective agency contacted Big Al. There was an announcement in the New York papers about Elizabeth Hamilton's upcoming wedding.

Chapter 40

December 2004

What is it about this girl that makes me think she had something to do with Mikey? He didn't know, but he never forgot the fact that on New Year's Eve, Elizabeth Hamilton was getting married to some other ballet guy. Big Al put it in the back of his mind.

After Christmas, the detective sent Big Al a copy of an article in the paper about that girl's rehearsal party and the published location of the wedding.

Big Al figured that if Elizabeth had anything to do with Mikey, and because of the fact that she was so beautiful, Mikey might show up for the wedding. He had a hunch. He didn't know why he thought he could have a chance to pay Mikey back for double-crossing him, but he had always followed his instincts, and they had not let him down yet.

He got to St. Raphael's Chapel early and waited. He watched from the organ loft. A harpist was playing music, so Big Al figured he was safe up in the loft. There weren't that many people, and no one came up into the loft area. He just crouched down and waited to see if his intuition was right.

She was one beautiful broad. He could see why the people in that town said she looked like she was floating when she walked. She glided down the aisle toward her groom. He had looked at every guest, and Mikey was not to be seen. He started to feel that his gut feelings had let him down as the ceremony came to a close. They were at the "Anyone object?" part when he heard the doors fly open and someone yell "Stop."

Big Al drew his pistol. Was this the chance he had been waiting for? Was he finally going to pay back Mikey for screwing him?

He got his answer very quickly because Michael Ryan started walking toward the altar. He passed directly under Big Al and then in front of Big Al. It was perfect. Big Al had a smile on his face when he pulled the trigger. He didn't want to hit the beautiful blonde. He had a soft spot for her. He just aimed at Mikey's back, pulled the trigger, and headed out the door.

"I got you, you bastard," he said as he left the church. He had gotten another gang member to have a car waiting just down the street from St. Raphael's. No one followed him. They were all in shock. He calmly walked down the street, got in the car, and left New York City.

Chapter 41

"You're a friend of the injured man?" asked the triage nurse.

"Yes, yes, I am," answered Elizabeth.

"Are you okay, ma'am?" she asked.

"I'm fine. I'm sorry. I'll change as soon as I can."

"I just wanted to make sure that you weren't injured. I'm sorry. Getting back to the victim, he's lost a lot of blood, and we've had to revive him twice. The doctors have sent him up for surgery. We just wondered if you knew of any family we could contact. His chances of surviving this injury are very slim."

Elizabeth was devastated. She could not hide her sorrow. It was immediately obvious that this man was not simply a friend or acquaintance.

"I don't think he has any living family," she told the nurse. "He told me that both of his parents were dead, and he doesn't have any brothers or sisters."

"Well, I'll tell that to the doctors. Would you like us to update you after the surgery?"

"Yes, yes, please."

Elizabeth barely got the words out. She could not believe what had happened. How could Michael Ryan come into her life again and disrupt it so much? He had already done that the first time he was injured. She spent her whole summer taking care of him for God's sake. Why? *And why does it mean so much to me?*

Elizabeth could not look at Peter. She felt so guilty—over the wedding, over the reception, over the obvious fact that Michael Ryan meant something to her. She didn't know what to say to him.

Monique had gone down to the little store in the hospital and bought Elizabeth a nurse's outfit. She wanted to get that blood-stained wedding gown off of her. She returned and coaxed Elizabeth into a washroom to change.

"Honey, how do you know this man? Please talk to me," she pleaded.

"Oh, Mom, what if he dies? What if he dies before I can talk to him?"

"And what could you possibly say to him that would make so much of a difference? Baby, it's your wedding day. Peter—what about Peter?"

"I don't know. I don't know. I thought I could pull it off."

"Pull it off? What do you mean pull it off?"

"I've had dreams for the last few weeks, and I've had trouble falling asleep. I was wondering why I should be troubled when the best part of my life was going to happen. I didn't figure it out until I saw Michael. Mom, Peter doesn't make my heart skip a beat. But my heart skipped a hundred beats when I saw Michael's face. Isn't it a great face? Doesn't he have the most beautiful eyes? Then I knew. I knew what was bothering me—Peter wasn't Michael."

"Who in the hell is Michael?"

"It's a long story, but his name is Michael Ryan. He was injured on the side of the road when I first went to the cottage, and I helped nurse him back to health. He was with me most of the time I was away."

"What? Why didn't you tell me?"

"I left that part back at the cottage. I didn't want to worry you. I thought you would be concerned about the whole thing, which I'll tell you about later."

"Honey."

"Right now I'm so worried Michael will die. But he's strong and stubborn, so I know he'll fight. Mom, what do I do about Peter? He's just sitting there staring at me. I can't bring myself to look him in the face. What should I do?"

"You have to be honest with Peter, honey. He deserves the truth. He's a good man. He really loves you. I'm not sure how he's going to deal with all of this."

"Mom, Michael told me he loves me in the ambulance. He loves me. Do you believe that?"

"I don't know what I believe right now. Why would this man tell you he loves you for God's sake? It's been months since you left the cottage, and you haven't mentioned him once."

"I thought it was all over. I thought I had lost him. But then he tells me he loves me. How great is that? I waited months to hear something even close to that statement come out of his mouth—because I love him too."

"What?"

"I love him. I knew it the minute I saw him. That's what I've been missing—Michael Ryan."

"Are you sure?"

"Positive. I've never been more positive of anything in my life. What will I do if he dies? Mom, he can't die—not until I tell him that I love him too."

"Oh, honey, I'm so sorry."

Both women returned to the waiting room. They put Elizabeth's beautiful gown in the garbage, wrapped in the bag the nurse's uniform came in.

Both men were silent in the waiting room. Monique and Elizabeth returned and sat down without saying a word. Elizabeth could not bring herself to look at Peter. No one spoke a word for two hours.

Peter broke the silence.

"Elizabeth, you have to explain this to me, please. I feel like I'm losing my mind. You're sitting there scared to death of losing someone who, to me, is a total stranger. We were seconds from being pronounced husband and wife for shit's sake, and in walks this guy, yelling stop, and then he gets shot. This is crazy."

"Peter, I'm so sorry."

"I don't want sorry, Elizabeth. I want an explanation. I deserve an explanation."

"You're right. You do. You do deserve an explanation. I think we should find a spot to talk."

Peter and Elizabeth found a corner on the hospital patio. Both looked drained and scared.

"I haven't told you how I've been feeling these last few weeks."

"What do you mean?"

"I haven't been sleeping, and I've been restless and losing my concentration. There's been something on my mind, but I couldn't figure it out. I was upset because it looked like I wasn't as happy as you, or so it seemed to me."

"Elizabeth, those are just prewedding jitters."

"No, no, I don't think so. You see, when I saw Michael at the bottom of that aisle, the jitters, as you called them, went away. I knew in that instant what was missing in my life."

Elizabeth went on to tell Peter what happened while she was away at the cottage. She told him about happening upon the beating, rescuing Michael Ryan, nursing him back to health, and falling in love with him.

"I'm sorry, Peter. I have to be honest. I owe you that much. You've been so wonderful to me. You're my best friend and my partner. But for some reason I can't explain, my heart belongs to someone else."

Peter sat with his head lowered and his shoulders slumped forward. He didn't want to hear what he was hearing, but he knew that she meant what she said. It was such a bizarre story that no one could make this up. He decided to leave and let Elizabeth and Monique deal with this guy. He had no feelings for him. He didn't want him to die, but then again, he didn't want him around period. He loved Elizabeth too much to add more stress to the situation.

Getting mad and creating a scene was not going to get Elizabeth's heart back. He could see by the look in her eyes that there was no doubt about who she loved. He had lost her, and it was time for him to leave and begin the healing process.

"Well, you know that I love you. I might always love you. I don't understand how this all happened and why I'm just hearing about this man now. But it is what it is. Thank you for telling me what happened. I wish you had told me sooner, but I'll trust you when you say that you didn't realize it until today. I think that it's time for me to leave and let you deal with this tragedy."

"Peter?"

"No. It's okay. I can't remove your feelings. I don't want to live with someone who cannot give herself to me completely. I'm going to go to the hotel, change, use one of our tickets, and leave New York. I really do have to be by myself right now."

"It was supposed to be our getaway. I'm so sorry, Peter."

"Elizabeth, please stop apologizing, please. I'll have the hotel hold onto your things, and you can make arrangements to get them back to your mother's apartment."

She reached for his shoulder. He put his hand over hers, removed it, and walked away. Elizabeth sat in the corner by herself, quietly crying. She could not believe what had happened in the last few hours. She had never wanted to hurt Peter. She did love him, but not with the passion she had for Michael Ryan. Her entire world had turned upside down. Now Michael was fighting for his life. *You've got to fight,* she thought. *I have to tell you how I feel. We have to have a chance to be together. You just have to fight . . . fight for us.*

Monique had told Jacques the entire story by the time Elizabeth returned from her talk with Peter.

"Where's Peter?" Monique asked.

"He left."

"Left?"

"Oh, Mom. I've made such a mess of things. I've hurt Peter terribly. He's going to go to Cuba alone. It was supposed to be our honeymoon. Why couldn't I just forget about Michael Ryan? Why couldn't I just live this perfect life I had here? Why?"

"Honey, I knew something was wrong; really, I did. I was wondering why I was more excited about this wedding than you seemed to be. I looked in your eyes these last few weeks and didn't see that usual sparkle—that sparkle that's there when you dance, that's there when you're excited or concentrating on something you love."

"I tried. I really did. If Michael hadn't walked into that church, we'd be having dinner right now, and I would have been quite content to live out that scene."

"Content—Elizabeth, that's not a word that should be said when someone just gets married. Ecstatic, overwhelmed, happy beyond words—these are feelings that should be in your heart. Your heart is telling you something, honey. Do you just want to be content?"

"No."

"So, let's sit here and pray that this young man doesn't want to be content either. He's going to have to fight like hell for his life, according to the doctors."

"Oh, Mom, he fought so hard last summer—really. I thought for sure he was going to die. I really did. I did everything in my power to help him heal, and he did. Maybe he'll just go back to that mindset and heal again. What do you think?"

"Maybe he will, sweetie, maybe he will. Let's just hope for the best."

They sat, waited, and hoped for the best for the next two hours. It was now 9:00 p.m. Jacques had gone to the hotel to announce that the wedding dinner would not be happening. He conveyed the apologies of the family. Maria and John said that they would handle any of the cancellations, the hotel staff, and any guests who happened to arrive late. Having performed those duties, he decided to get something to eat and some coffee. Elizabeth couldn't eat, but they convinced her to at least have a cup of coffee. Her stomach was turning, her mind was reeling, and her heart was aching.

Chapter 42

Detective Paul James had been called to the church to check on a shooting.

On New Year's Eve for Christ's sake. You'd think people could stop killing each other for just one night.

When he arrived at the church, there were signs of a definite shooting. Blood was all over the aisle. *Yup, there was a shooting all right.*

The cops that had arrived on the scene had questioned a few of the guests to find out what happened. James could not believe that someone tried to knock someone off at a wedding. *What next?* he thought.

Well, it seemed that luck was on the good guys' side tonight. The wedding photographer had turned when the shot rang out and looked up to the loft. His camera kept clicking. "It was instinct," he said. The photographer said that he had started off as a newspaper photographer, and instinct took over. He saw a story, and he just clicked. The guy had taken pictures of the shooter.

Big Al had reacted to the situation with his emotions and not his brain. He should have known that there would be photographers and people with cameras at a wedding.

But he had focused solely on attaining his revenge. This mistake would cost him.

The beat cops had taken the camera to the precinct to get the pictures downloaded into the police files. James was waiting for the report when he went to the hospital.

The threesome didn't know that the police had been called about the shooting and an investigation had begun. Since they were not family, the police had left them alone, but now it was time to question the people that the detective thought were personally involved with the victim. He figured that the shooting had something to do with the bride.

Jesus, she looks like shit, he thought as he approached the three people involved with the wedding. *Whoa, that groom is a little old for that young girl.*

"Hello, folks, sorry to bother you at a time like this, but we have an attempted murder here."

Everyone looked up. No one said anything.

"My name is Paul James. I'm a detective with the New York Police Department. I'm in charge of the investigation." James put his hand out to shake Jacques' hand.

"Jacques Beaubien," he said. "And this is Monique Hamilton and her daughter, Elizabeth."

"Hello. I'm wondering, Mr. uh Beaubien, if you think you were the target instead of this guy who interrupted your wedding."

"What?"

"Well, it looks like a sort of lover's triangle going on here. Someone didn't want you to marry your fiancé."

"Me. No, Monsieur, I am not the groom. I am the escort of the bride's mother. I am Madame Hamilton's confidante and her partner. Elizabeth is like my daughter. Peter Rogers is the groom."

"Peter Rogers. Well, where is he?"

"I'm afraid he has left the hospital, and he is probably on his way to Cuba by now."

"Cuba?"

"Yes, he and Elizabeth were to be going there on their honeymoon, and Mr. Rogers has been, shall we say, left at the altar, so he decided to go alone to Cuba."

"Oh, well we'll have to get him back to New York, it looks like."

"Peter had nothing to do with this," Elizabeth said as she stood up. "This has nothing to do with Peter. Peter doesn't know Michael, and Peter needs to be left alone. He has suffered enough. Please do not bother Peter in Cuba. The least he can have is peace."

"Well, Miss . . ."

"Hamilton."

"Miss Hamilton—he's part of this whole situation here, and we may have to get him back to New York to conclude the investigation."

Elizabeth sighed and sat back down. There wasn't much more she could take. She was dying inside. The doctors had not updated them since Michael went into surgery. She was starting to lose control, and she was doing everything within her to keep herself together.

"Now, could one of you give your version of the scene that occurred at St. Raphael's?"

Monique decided to speak up. She was trying to get the focus off of Elizabeth. She knew Elizabeth had been stretched to her limit. She told Detective James her version of the events, and they seemed to jell with what the people at the church has described. He was trying to figure out what this guy, Michael Ryan, had to do with the wedding party.

"We checked the ID in the victim's pocket, and his name is Michael Ryan. His address is one from Connecticut. Which one of you, if any of you, knows the victim?"

"It's me," said Elizabeth. "I know Michael. He's my friend. We were acquaintances last summer. I don't know how he found out about the wedding, and I don't know why anyone would shoot him." She knew that she couldn't let on that he was a member of a bike gang. She didn't want Michael to get into trouble for things done in the past. She didn't know what had occurred since last summer. She was certain that the person who shot Michael was a member of that bike gang. She wondered how long it would take the police to find that out.

James had been told about the tattoos on Michael's arms and had been surprised that a man linked to the Mid Town Boys would be involved with a ballet dancer.

This girl has to be really stupid, naïve, or lying, he thought.

"Why did he interrupt your wedding?"

"To tell me he loves me."

"What?"

"To tell me he loves me. You see, Detective, last summer, Michael and I were together for quite a long time, and we developed a friendly relationship. Well, it seems that Michael developed love toward me but never told me. He came to the wedding to tell me. He wanted me to know before I got married."

"And?"

"And in the ambulance, he told me. I'm not sure how he found me because we didn't exchange any personal information. But he did. Detective, it seems that I love him back. That's why my fiancé is now on his way to Cuba alone. We didn't get married. And now some crazy person enters the church during my wedding and shoots someone. This is crazy."

"Crazy things happen, Miss Hamilton."

A uniformed police officer approached the group and motioned to James to come to him. When James approached him, they spoke in whispers for a few minutes, and then the officer handed James a brown envelope.

"Well, it seems that we've had quite a bit of luck in this case. Your wedding photographer seems to have been in the right place at the right time. He happened to have the instinct to keep his camera clicking during the whole incident. We have a picture of the shooter."

He showed the three of them a picture of Big Al. "Do any of you know this man or recognize him?"

All three of them said, "No."

"Well, this guy has a police record. We identified him through our files. How lucky is that? There's a picture of him taking aim on this Michael guy, so we have a great case against him. His name is Allan Kollinski. He's a known leader of a bike gang. He's had some brushes with the law; nothing put him away, however. He has a long list of arrests but no convictions. He was nailed for a few driving offenses, but no one has been able to convict this guy. We have a bulletin out for his arrest right now."

Elizabeth panicked a little. *I wonder if they will connect Michael with this Allan person,* she thought. *Now they might arrest Michael for his connection to this gang, as if he hasn't had enough trouble.*

"We also ran a check on the victim. He had a few scraps when he was a juvenile, but we have nothing on him since then. It seems he's pretty clean. Someone's going to the address on his driver's license to check on any family."

"I don't think he has a family," Elizabeth said. "I remember him telling me that both of his parents had died and that he didn't have any siblings."

"Well, we're gonna check that out. In the meantime, please try to think of a reason that a leader of a bike gang would come to your church and shoot someone who just wanted to stop the wedding. Why would Al Kollinski shoot Michael Ryan?"

Chapter 43

A doctor in surgical scrubs finally appeared around 11:30 p.m. Detective James approached him first.

"Doc, I'm Detective James. I'm in charge of the investigation concerning your patient."

"Detective James. Well, I don't know where this guy gets his strength, but he managed to pull through the surgery. He's not out of the woods by any stretch of the imagination. He had lost so much blood that we almost ran out of blood to give him. Like I say, he's getting strength from somewhere and God knows where. He's heavily sedated. It was a long operation. I don't figure he'll be awake for another hour or so. And then I don't know how long he'll actually last."

Elizabeth's heart just about stopped beating. Monique squeezed her hand and put her arm around Elizabeth's shoulders. Elizabeth couldn't even speak. She was trembling and felt like she would pass out. *He could die,* she thought. *He could die before I tell him that I love him too. Why did I let him leave the cottage? Why didn't I stop him then? This wouldn't have happened. Peter wouldn't have been so hurt. And Michael wouldn't be fighting to stay alive. Can his body endure this much damage, so soon after last summer?*

"This guy had quite a beating fairly recently. We found a lot of internal tissue that's still healing from some sort of trauma. It looks like he was in some kind of accident. He has scars and tissue damage all over his body. This guy is used to fighting for his life, I think."

"Yeah," said James. "Maybe that's connected to the shooting in some way. We've identified the shooter and have an APB out for him. He's probably out of the state by now, but this is an interstate bulletin. We should get some bites soon on his whereabouts."

"Well, finding the shooter won't help my patient. He needs to focus on himself, so I would hope that if you speak to him, it's very brief, and then you leave him alone. I don't know how much more his body or his psyche can take."

Elizabeth stood up and walked toward the doctor. "Doctor, my name is Elizabeth Hamilton, and I'm a very good friend of Michael Ryan."

Everyone was staring at her.

"It's a little hard for me to say it out loud that I love him, but I should have realized it and said it much sooner than tonight. Michael told me that he loved me in the ambulance. Is it possible for me to sit with him? You were right. He did have an accident last summer, and I was with him while he convalesced. Maybe I can help him again. I know I can help again. Please."

"We can't have anyone with him until he comes out of the recovery room. We have to make sure that he's stabilized. Once we get him out of danger, then I'm sure we can arrange for you to see him."

"After me," stated James.

"Okay, Detective, after you. I'm sure we can get both of you to see him if he makes it through the next hour or so."

Elizabeth didn't want to hear "if he makes it through the next hour or so." She wanted to be told that he would heal, that he would will himself back to health one more time. *Come on, Michael, fight—just fight.*

Chapter 44

Monique and Jacques went back to the apartment to change and try to get some sleep. Bringing Elizabeth a new change of clothes and some toiletries would help Elizabeth feel better. Elizabeth would also benefit from the support of two people who were rested and refreshed. They left the hospital reluctantly, but they knew that Elizabeth may now need some time alone.

Elizabeth would not budge from the waiting room. She was waiting for the doctor to tell her that she could see Michael, and she wasn't going anywhere.

She waited alone and in silence. She played back the scene at the chapel over and over in her head. She saw his beautiful blue eyes looking at her and his arms outstretched toward her. Her heart had skipped a beat when she had turned toward his voice. It gave her comfort to visualize the look in his eyes. She was trying to block out the blood and the sound of the heart monitor going flat.

At 2:30 a.m., the doctor came out and told Detective James that they were moving Michael out of the recovery room into Intensive Care. He had managed to survive and was now semiconscious.

James moved immediately toward Intensive Care. Elizabeth got up and looked at the doctor. She was petrified. She looked exhausted and drained.

"You know, Miss Hamilton, it might be a good idea for you to go home and get some rest. You really aren't looking good right now."

"I'm not going anywhere, Doctor. I will not be leaving this hospital. Is it possible for me to see Michael after the police finish talking to him? I promise I'll say one sentence, and then I'll just sit and hold his hand."

The doctor smiled. He knew exactly what sentence she was talking about. She had made that perfectly clear earlier on in the evening.

"As soon as Detective James finishes with him, yes, you can go in and sit with him. Now I have to go in and make sure that Detective James does not upset him or put stress on his heart. If you'll excuse me."

Elizabeth sat down with a thud. Her legs felt like rubber. They were always the strongest part of her body, but right now they felt like the weakest. The few minutes she waited for Detective James to return seemed like years.

"Well, I didn't get much out of him," he said. "He's still out of it. All he kept saying was Liz. That would be you, wouldn't it?"

Elizabeth got up quickly. "I'm going in to see him now."

"I'll be getting back to him. You don't have to say anything to him right now. I know he won't be going anywhere anytime soon. But I have to find out the connection between him and this Allan guy. I hope he makes it through, Miss Hamilton. Good luck."

She stood at the door to the Intensive Care ward. Michael was in the first bed. There were tubes and machines everywhere. A nurse was checking on machines, so she waited until the nurse was finished to approach the bed.

He looks so helpless, even worse than last summer. Maybe it's because he has no beard and ponytail. She smiled. His eyes were closed, and he wasn't moving. *Please move, Michael, so that I know you're alive. Just move.*

The nurse finished up her duties, gave Elizabeth a nod, and left. Elizabeth moved closer to the bed. She was moving so slowly. She did not want to wake him. She couldn't resist and touched his hand.

Elizabeth put her head down on the bed and started crying. It was a soft, low sob that came from the depths of her soul. She let some of the stress of the last twelve hours or so escape her body. Without realizing it, she fell asleep. Exhaustion took over, and she fell asleep holding Michael Ryan's hand.

The loud din sounded far, far away to Elizabeth. She didn't realize what was happening until a nurse grabbed her shoulders and asked her to leave. She thought that the sound was part of a dream, but reality soon shocked her. Michael had stopped breathing.

"Please wait outside, Miss. We need the room."

Elizabeth stumbled into the hallway. Doctors and nurses were rushing to the ICU, and the sound of the heart monitor was just about causing her heart to stop. She could hear the alarming conversation between the doctors and nurses.

"Michael, you can't leave me now. I haven't told you. I need you to at least know that I return your love. Please, please . . ."

There were two more episodes of the heart monitor showing a straight line and producing the dreaded resonance that meant that Michael's heart had stopped beating. The doctors had managed to revive Michael two more times. His heart had beaten normally for about ten minutes when the nurses and doctors started leaving the ICU. The ICU nurse approached Elizabeth.

"He's unbelievably fighting to live. With so much blood loss and the severity of the tissue damage, he could have given up a long time ago. Something is keeping this man battling death. You can go in, but please let him rest and allow him to heal."

Barely breathing, Elizabeth whispered, "Thank you. I won't disturb him. Thank you so much for saving him. Michael is a fighter. Thank you."

Her legs were barely able to keep her standing and walking. She was trembling with fear and sadness. She could not believe how pathetic he looked. There was no color in his face. He had been to hell and back. She took the chair and moved it beside his bed and gently touched his hand and stared into the face of the man she so loved. She prayed that she would get the chance to tell him that she loved him.

I'll help you get better again. Please, Michael. Please.

Time went by slowly in the hospital. Elizabeth changed and got some rest while Monique took her place beside the bed.

Michael had not regained consciousness since the last CPR incident. The doctors had told her that it was common for the mind to turn itself off to allow the body to heal and that the longer Michael stayed alive, the greater the chance there was for him to wake up.

It was difficult to wait.

Elizabeth had started to talk to him. She believed that if he could hear her, it would motivate him to wake up. Reminiscing about their days at the cottage was the major focus of her talks. She told him over and over again that she loved him. She begged him to fight his way back to health.

Someone's holding my hand. I've felt that touch before. I know that softness. Where the hell am I? I can't move. Am I dreaming?

Elizabeth thought she felt a movement in Michael's hand. She immediately started crying.

"Michael, Michael. Can you hear me? Please, Michael. Wake up. Wake up. I want you to open your eyes. I have to tell you that I love you. Please, Michael."

Who's that? She loves me? Who's that? It sounds like Elizabeth. Elizabeth? How could it be Elizabeth? Okay, now, Mikey, if this is her, you have to hang in there and wake up. Wake up.

Elizabeth couldn't take her eyes off of Michael's face. She was looking for any indication that he was regaining consciousness. Time was going by so slowly. Did she imagine his finger moving?

"I love you so much, Michael Ryan. You have to wake up so that I can tell you. Michael. Come back to me. Michael."

She could barely breathe through her sobs. She had laid her head down on the bed. She was so tired, but she would not leave him alone. She was whimpering when a hand landed on her head.

Elizabeth jumped up and stared into two slightly open blue eyes—the most beautiful blue eyes she had ever seen.

"Hello, beautiful."

Elizabeth didn't get the chance to reply or react. She fainted and slid onto the floor.

Chapter 45

January 2005

Big Al had been discovered in a bar not far from the bikers' safe house. It had not been a little difficult to weed him out. Bikers are usually very loyal to each other.

Detective James would not give up on the investigation and had managed to find a biker that had a grudge against Big Al. You don't make it to the top of a bike gang without making enemies. Squirrel, the traitor, had given James a lead on Big Al's location. He was hiding out and was really pissed that Mike had survived once again. He couldn't believe that the two bullets he put into Mike's back hadn't killed him.

James had watched the house for days, and finally Big Al took the chance to leave the house. He walked down the street with a group of bikers around him to the local bar. He had been going crazy holed up in that house.

The SWAT unit had the bar surrounded, and James held up the bullhorn announcing that the place was surrounded and that Big Al should just give himself up.

Big Al had no intention of going quietly with these cops. There was no way he was going to get put in jail for that bastard. He believed that he would get out of the mess he was in. The police waited for someone to come out of the bar with their hands up, but it didn't occur. They moved closer to the bar, smashed a window, and threw in a smoke bomb. The bikers eventually starting rushing out of the bar, coughing and collapsing. Big Al staying inside as long as he possibly could bear the smoke. He had decided not to give up without a fight. If he went out firing, he may be able to make the cops duck, and then he could run to safety. Much to Big Al's bad luck, the SWAT team members were behind shields and did not have to duck from the bullets Big Al was shooting. He was shot dead as soon as he came out the door. The saga was over. No one would ever know why Big Al had chosen to shoot Mike. No one would ever know that Mike had been a member of the same bike gang. The secret died with Big Al.

Chapter 46

May 2005

It was exactly one year to the day that Michael Ryan had endured the beating of his life. That seemed like light years ago. He was standing in the back room of the town chapel. He was wearing the first tuxedo of his life. His heart was beating a million beats per minute. Jacques had brought him a big glass of wine, but it didn't help calm him down. He was jumping out of his skin with excitement. It had been a whirlwind few months.

"I appreciate you standing up for me, Jacques."

"It is a pleasure to accompany you on this most special day. Please let us drink and make a toast to a beautiful and peaceful day."

"Peaceful . . . yeah. How's Elizabeth doing? You don't think she'd change her mind, do you?"

"Change her mind. *Non, mon ami,* I have never seen a woman so ready to get married. Her eyes are shining, and her heart is smiling."

Michael smiled.

Elizabeth had stayed by his side for two months. He had been in the hospital for three weeks and then moved to Monique's apartment. Elizabeth, again, had nursed him back to health. A nurse came in periodically to check on his progress, but considering everything he had been through, Mike had healed completely.

Jacques convinced Monique to get married. The events of the New Year had convinced her that life was meant to be lived and not wasted. She had come to the conclusion that life was too special and that she should just grab the reigns and go for it.

April Fool's Day was an odd choice, but it was a most special day for the Hamiltons and the Beaulieus.

There was something special about being in Paris in April. Hyacinths were everywhere inside Jacques' home and outside in the small garden. There was only family present, but the couple did not want to wait. They had waited too long, and they both realized how life changed in a blink.

So, on April 1, Monique and Jacques got married in Paris. It was a very small ceremony. Jacques's son was his best man, and Michael Ryan was an attendant. Elizabeth was the maid of honor, and Jacques's daughter was an attendant.

Elizabeth now had a brother and sister, and she was ecstatic. She was so happy for her mother. She had worked so hard her entire life to make Elizabeth happy. Now it was her turn.

"I'm glad you retired, Mom."

"Me too, dear. Life is too short."

Monique had retired from the magazine in March, and she and Jacques had moved her possessions to Paris. They both loved the city, and Monique knew that Elizabeth would be fine with Michael Ryan in New York City.

"How is life going in Paris?"

"I love Paris. I love New York too. But now Paris is my home with my husband. Do you believe it—husband? This is so wonderful. And now you will get that feeling too, honey. This is a special day."

"It is."

"Have you heard anything from Peter?"

"Peter returned from Cuba and began rehearsing for the upcoming ballet. I pulled out of the production. I opted to take care of Michael. Peter and his new partner had a very successful opening. The new production was a success. Michael and I attended the opening."

Michael felt guilty, but Elizabeth had ensured him that all was fine and that there would be other productions in the future. Peter and Elizabeth did not really speak any more, but they acknowledged each other in public. Peter's wound had been too deep. It was rumored that he had begun a relationship with his new partner, but nothing had been made public.

It was getting close to the time to start the wedding. Jacques and Michael were in the groom's side of the church.

Elizabeth was with Monique at the other end of the small church. They had decided to get married in the church of the town where everything happened. They were five miles from the cottage where their love had developed. They had come full circle in one year. The date was chosen because of its significance—May 3.

Her wedding dress, this time, was a soft off-white chiffon gown. She was wearing ballet slippers again. Her feet loved ballet slippers. She let her hair fall down over her shoulders. She had a simple flower in her hair and Gram's pearls around her neck. She looked beautiful.

"You look so beautiful, honey. This time, I do see that sparkle. Your eyes are sparkling so much that I'm almost blinded."

They both laughed.

"I'm so happy, Mom. It feels right this time. I have no doubts, no regrets. He's the one I want to spend the rest of my life with. He's the love of my life. I can feel Gram smiling down on us right now. I did what she said; I followed my heart."

"Gram was an authority on one following his or her heart, wasn't she?"

"Yes, she was. She had told me that just a few days before she died. How she knew that it was exactly what I needed to hear, I'll never know. But she knew."

"She always knew. So, my sweetie, shall we get this show started?"

Again, the *Moonlight Sonata* started, and Monique escorted Elizabeth down the aisle. Jacques was standing next to Michael. Pierre, Jacques's son, was in attendance next to Jacques. Jacqueline, Elizabeth's new sister, was waiting on the left side of the altar. Maggie was also there.

Mike had adopted her as family. All eyes were on the two women walking slowly toward the altar.

Michael Ryan inhaled and let his breath out slowly. *How can I guy like me be so lucky to be hooking up with a girl like her?* He thanked his lucky stars and watched his beautiful bride come toward him.

Tears were flowing down her cheeks, and her eyes were sparkling. She couldn't keep her eyes off of Michael. *I'm so lucky,* she thought. *I'm so lucky to be marrying a man that I truly love.*

The ceremony did not take long. Then the preacher made the problematic statement, "If anyone here has any objections to this marriage, let them now speak or forever hold their peace."

Everyone held his or her breath. Not a sound was heard in the small chapel. Then everyone started to laugh.

"Well then, if no one objects, I now pronounce you husband and wife."

Michael Ryan took his bride into his arms and kissed her passionately for the entire world to see.

This time, no party had been planned. Michael and Elizabeth walked happily out of the chapel to the waiting car. Elizabeth kissed her mother and stepfather good-bye. Monique and Elizabeth had an extra-long hug, and then Elizabeth turned and entered the waiting car. Everyone waved and yelled congratulations, and then the car was out of sight.

The car traveled through town, down the highway, and into Cottage Lane. When it got to Connie Hamilton's cottage drive, the car turned.

Elizabeth and Michael thanked the driver, and the car drove away. The newlyweds stood before the front door and closed their eyes and listened to the sounds. They could hear the animals, the birds, the lake, and the wind. They smiled at each other.

"We're home," Michael said.

With that, he swept Elizabeth into his arms and walked up the steps. They fumbled to get the door open, which made them both laugh. The door finally opened, and Michael carried his bride over the threshold.

Michael Ryan and Elizabeth Ryan then closed the door to the cottage.

About the Author

Donna Marchand Vamplew, a proud French Acadian, was born in Sydney, Nova Scotia. After twenty-four years teaching English, business, and physical education at Toronto's Notre Dame High School, where she also served as a guidance counselor and coach, she retired. She and her husband of thirty-three years have two adult children. This is her debut novel, and she is currently at work on her second novel, titled Haunted Castle.

See an exciting excerpt from her upcoming book on the next page.

iUniverse Publishing
proudly presents

HAUNTED CASTLE

by

Donna Vamplew

Turn the page for a preview of
HAUNTED CASTLE . . .

Chapter 1

The gunshots were becoming a little too close for comfort! Charley O'Neil, Liam Clancy's partner went ahead of him in the alley.

They had been having a bite to eat; when the call came through that, some gunfire was heard just down the street from where they were eating.

Down went the half-eaten sandwiches and each took a last sip of coffee before they bolted out of the restaurant.

They both screamed, "We'll be back Sally to square up".

"No problem", replies Sally. She shakes her head as the two men run out of her restaurant. She loved having the police officers frequent her restaurant every day. She felt like she was helping the city in some sort of way. Liam Clancy's father had been one of her customers for 40 years. She closed her eyes and said a silent prayer that God would keep them safe.

So, as usual, the two best friends take off to check it out. It was not their call. Nevertheless, they were constantly on alert for action. In addition, they were always sticking their noses into things that did not concern them. "Two peas in a pod", people used to say, about these two Irish boys from the East Side.

"Don't get too far ahead of me, partner", called out Liam.

Then, it happens again. Charley steps out from behind the dumpster. Shouts ring out. Charley crashes against the dumpster; blood is all over the place.

Liam runs towards Charley screaming, "No, no!" Liam hears a noise to his left. Liam turns and fires. A ten-year-old boy hits the ground. Charley looks down at his hands. There is blood all over his hands. Liam drops the gun and turns to look at Charley.

As Liam turns, he wakes up sweating profusely. *"When is this nightmare gonna stop? When? When?"*

There were so many images and sounds that Liam could not erase from his mind—the shots, Charley's blood, Charley's face, the boy's blood, the boy's body face down in the alley. It had been 6 months, since that night. He had not returned to work and he had not had a full night's sleep since that night.

The investigation into the shooting of the boy had been tense. Liam swore that he thought the kid had a gun in his hand. No one found a gun.

"He had his hand in his pocket", Liam had told the investigating Detective. "I saw a bulge and I shot. I didn't even realize that it was a kid. We're talking about seconds. It was seconds between my getting to Charley and my turning to the sound in the alley. I thought whoever shot Charley was taking aim to shoot me."

Liam was cleared of all charges, but it did not take away his guilt. It did not take away the pain of losing his partner.

He had wished it was he who had died in that alley, that night. Charley had two young kids and a beautiful wife. Now, she was a widow and the boys would grow up without a father.

Every night, Liam would sit after his nightmare and chastise himself for not dying that evening. He would cry and he would take a gulp of whiskey, in hopes that it would help him get back to sleep. It really didn't. He was, in his mind, experiencing the living dead.

Chapter 2

Liam Clancy had not been able to go back to work. The thought of killing anyone made him nauseous, especially any kid! He was now relegated to the Precinct Office, helping out with the paper work and the organization of the Precinct.

The Chief of Police, Jack Clancy, watched his son go through the motions of living for months and wondered when and how Liam would crawl out of the hole, he had dug for himself.

Liam had returned to the Clancy home after the shooting. There now were three people in a home, where there used to be 6 kids and two parents. Maeve Clancy had been the proud bearer of six boys. After three boys, she continued trying to get herself a girl, but after a set of twin boys, she gave up.

Jimmy was the oldest (James Jr.). He was a beat cop. He did not want to be anything else. He did not want to move up the ladder to become a detective. He was a Sergeant in the same Precinct his father had commanded. He was proud to follow in "Big Jack's Shoes".

Patrick was next. He was a doctor. He had not followed the family legacy of police work. He ran the Emergency

Department at County General, loving the fast paced and stressful environment. He was not the same as all the other Clancy's; saving lives instead of possibly ending lives. He had been at the hospital when Charley was brought in to Emerg. He knew when he looked at him that nothing could be done to save Charley's life. They had tried to revive Charley twice in the ambulance, but it was too late. One of the bullets had ripped straight through his heart. Patrick was devastated that he could not help Charley and even more shattered that he had to tell his brother that his best friend was gone.

Liam was the third born. His goal was to be a cop from the moment he was born. He only finished high school because he had to graduate in order to apply to Police College. He was at the top of his graduating class from the Police Academy. He was a gung ho, no holds barred, type of cop. He loved it. He had become a detective in four years, which raised a few eyebrows. Then, he was partnered with his life-long friend Charley O'Neil. For Liam, he had the perfect life. He had been dating a beautiful, blonde-haired woman named Sam. They had been together for six months, which was a record for Liam.

Bobby was only 10 months younger than Liam. Mrs. Clancy had been a busy woman; not mentioning Jack's role in the family planning! Bobby was also a cop. However, Bobby had gone down a different path in Law Enforcement. His expertise was forensics. He was slowly getting a Forensics Degree as he was working as a beat cop. In no time at al, l Patrick would be finished his forensic education.

Working in the Medical Examiner's Office was his goal. He was the "brains" of the family, along with Patrick.

Bringing up the rear was a set of twins, Sean and Kieran. Sean was so named because he almost did not make it through the first hour of his life. He was a fighter. Maeve had named her fifth son with this name, as it meant, "favored one". She figured God had favored this child at birth and had pulled him through his rocky beginnings. Kieran had black hair—the dark one. All her other sons had light brown hair and her last born had jet-black hair! These two would be trouble, she had said to herself after their birth.

This made up the Clancy Family. Maeve, James Sr., James Jr. (Jimmy), Patrick (Patty), William (Liam), Robert (Bobby), Sean and Kieran practically filled up a whole church pew on Sundays. They were the Clancy Clan and they were proud of their heritage. In true Irish tradition, most of the Clan became police officers. Sean and Kieran had been late comers to the brood. There were six years between Bobby and the twins. They were both at College—separate ones. Sean was following Patrick's footsteps and had decided on medicine. He had always been an excellent student. He was interested in opening up his own general practice and becoming the quintessential family doctor. Kieran was a jock. He had managed to get himself a football scholarship at Notre Dame and he was in heaven. He just hoped that he could stay in school long enough to snag himself a professional career. School had not been one of Kieran's strong points. He liked to play.

All the boys had the same middle name—Ryan. It was the name of Maeve's father. As they grew up, you could hear this name being said when Maeve Clancy had reached her limit. You would hear, "Robert Ryan Clancy, you come down here immediately" and more often than not, "Sean Ryan, I want to speak to you now". She had her hands full while Jack went off to work as a police officer, climbing slowly up the department ladder. The boys adored their mother. No one dared do anything or say anything to Maeve Clancy that was out of order. Her boys walked beside her through life.

Chapter 3

Chief James no longer had his office in the 42nd Precinct. His son, Jimmy was a Sergeant there now. Liam was now doing paper work at the 42nd. The Chief did not like to see that, but he knew that Liam had to conquer the demons that were after him. He knew the demons. He had been attacked by them himself at different time in his career; he had lived with them and he had conquered them a few times himself. It is the part of police work, which no one talks about—how you deal with the crap that you see every day and how you deal with killing another human being.

He was having a battle with Liam because he would not attend the counseling sessions. After a departmental investigation, a police officer cannot retire to duty unless he attends therapy sessions and gets a green light from the therapist.

James was disturbed that Liam did not really care if he went back on the streets. But, was he was happy inside? Liam was not talking to anyone about the pain inside his heart. James wanted to help Liam get over this hurdle in his life, but he knew all too well that Liam had to initiate the healing. He knew that Liam was too far down in the pain right now to start crawling back up to reality.

Chapter 4

The Mayor was calling James Clancy.

"Shit", he thought. *"What the hell does he want?"*

It was a strange conversation. It seemed that "someone in the know" had called "someone in the know", and then someone with power called the Mayor. Being the Mayor of Los Angeles was not easy, on a good day. There were the gangs, the crime, and the poverty and of course, the movie stars. He had to please the movie stars as they carried a lot of power at election time. If you really pissed off a movie star, it could cost you your job.

Someone had asked the Mayor to assign a bodyguard to a rock group that would be headlining a big benefit concert at the Hollywood Bowl. The group was coming into the city early to record a new album and someone had threatened a member of the group. The Mayor, always on the side of pleasing the stars and the press, wanted James to find someone to fill this position. He didn't want any bad press happening in his city.

"What am I now", he thought, *"a goddamned babysitter for rockers?"*

"Mr. Mayor, I'm sure that these people can afford their own security detail." James was pleading now.

"You don't seem to understand", said the Mayor. "This is, one, a special request from a special person. And, two, a life was threatened and police presence is indeed. You have to make sure that an investigation into this threat is initiated. Are we clear?"

"Yes, sir. Crystal clear. I will get on it right away."

"That's what I like to hear. You have two weeks to set this up. And make sure you make those rockers happy."

James nodded and sighed.

Nevertheless, part of his job WAS to make sure that the Mayor was happy. He reluctantly started to look for someone to fill the bill. He only had a few years left before retiring. He could have retired four or five years prior, but he wanted to try out what being Chief of Police would be like. He wanted to make a statement with the Department— leave a legacy, inspire tradition and honesty within the Force that had given him so much for over the past 45 years.

James would have to look for someone who did know security systems in buildings and security at events. He also needed someone that could handle crowds and could handle himself in a fight. This person would also have to be able to boss around other people; a good authority figure type guy. The doings of rock groups were varied and crazy. Going with the punches and dodging the punches were necessary skills in this assignment.

"But what good cop wants to baby sit *a bunch of stupid rockers"*, he thought. *"No one in their right mind would want this position."* Then it struck him—no one in their right mind—Liam! Maybe this is what he needed to get

away from the Precinct and the paper work. He would wear a gun, but the odds of using it would be extremely low. He would have other people with guns that he would empower to shoot, if necessary. Having countless contacts in the Police World is something Liam held in spades. He would also know many retired cops and cops that had started their own security businesses to help him make sure this group of spoiled stars is kept safe. *"But how do I convince him to take the job?"* he asked himself.

To say that Liam was the stubborn son, was an understatement. Maeve Clancy always said that Liam "would be the death of me". Convincing him to take on this type of assignment was going to take a miracle. James also had to jolt him away from the comfort of the Precinct Office and into the real world—well almost the real world.

"42nd Precinct. Yes, Mrs. Campbell, yes we received your report about the hooligans in the playground last night. We're looking into the matter. No, no we haven't caught anyone yet, but we're close. Yes, we have it in the report, Mrs. Margaret Campbell, yes. Well, we try! Thank you. I'm sure you'll hear in the neighborhood if we catch those hooligans for you."

Mike was ready to scream. When you are stuck inside the Precinct building, you have to deal with the little, itty-bitty things of the neighborhood. You did not have to think much; you just had to make the people happy. He missed being outside in the middle of investigations, but the thought of it all scared him to death.

"42nd Precinct. Oh, hi Dad. What are you up to?

"The question is, my boy, what are you up to?"

"Well, let's see now. Mrs. Campbell called again today to check on the status of the hooligan investigation. It seems there were some hooligans in the playground night before last, after midnight, making a ruckus."

"Yes, well I've heard of those hooligans. They're usually about 15 to 18 years old and they do strange things like drink beer and play on the swings. I don't know what this world is coming to. As Chief, I want you to make sure that someone is on top of it. After all, we want Mrs. Campbell not to call the Precinct for at least two days. It looks like nothing has changed in the East Side".

"Nope, same old, same old."

"I was wondering it you'd have lunch with me today; on me"?

"On you? Well, glad to hear that the Police Department can afford to pay for my lunch. What's up?"

"Nothing much. I just wanted to pass something by you that came up today. The Mayor gave me one of those lovely little chores of his, I wanted some input, and I chose you. That's all."

"Well, if the Mayor is involved, I wouldn't want to let him down. You know what I think of him."

"Yes I do and you'll keep that to yourself, young man".

Liam let out a husky laugh. The heads of all the people in the lobby turned and looked at him. That was the usual reaction to Liam's laugh—it was contagious, loud and full of mischief.

James loved Liam's laugh and had not heard much of it in the past few months. It made him smile.

"I'll be there, Dad. Name the place."

"How about O'Toole's at 1:00 o'clock?"

"Great, see you then."

Chapter 5

August 2006

"I've gotta make sure that she doesn't find out what's going on", he thought. *"I don't know who in the hell this sicko is, but I'm gonna make damn sure that he doesn't get near to her."*

Peter had told Tommy to call someone in Los Angeles to set up a fake bodyguard. Jenny would not fall very easily for a fake story, so they had to be careful. Someone was sending her weird and psychotic mail. There had even been pictures, which demonstrated that the weirdo had infiltrated security in various cities. This depraved person was following them. Peter had come up with a plan. He said that they would hire someone to be the new Head of Security for LA. This individual would be a real cop and he would investigate the existence of this psychotic stalker while pretending to be the head of security for the group. They did not want Jenny to know that someone was following her. No one was to get near to her and Peter wanted to make sure of that. Keeping Jenny stress free and safe had been his goal for many years and now, there was a new danger!

Being forced to stay in London because his wife was pregnant was extremely upsetting to Peter. He was torn between a rock and a hard place. Tommy had advised him that there was a weird stalker following the band around. Other than Evelyn, his wife, Jenny was the most important thing in his life. Peter would give his life to protect Jenny, which he had already done in the past. There would soon be three important things in his life—Evelyn, the baby and Jenny. He was handling the problem from England and it made him very nervous that anyone would be remotely close to hurting Jenny.